Praise for *Fatal Forgery*

"I loved the sense of place, with some surprising revelations about jail and courthouse conditions and operations, and an interesting change of setting at one point, which I won't reveal for fear of spoiling the plot. There was great attention to detail woven skilfully into the writing, so I felt I learned a lot about the era by osmosis, rather than having it thrust upon me. All in all, a remarkable debut novel."
Debbie Young, author and book blogger, UK Ambassador for the Alliance of Independent Authors

"From the start of this story I felt as if I had been transported back in time to Regency London. Walking in Sam's footsteps, I could hear the same cacophony of sound, shared the same sense of disbelief at Fauntleroy's modus operandi, and hung onto Constable Plank's coat tails as he entered the squalid house of correction at Coldbath Fields. I am reassured that this is not the last we shall see of Samuel Plank. His steadfastness is so congenial that to spend time in his company in future books is a treat worth savouring."
Jo at Jaffareadstoo, Amazon "Top 500 Reviewer"

Praise for *The Man in the Canary Waistcoat*

"Having read the first Sam Plank novel and really enjoyed it I was so looking forward to the next, and 'The Man in the Canary Waistcoat' did not disappoint. Susan Grossey is an excellent storyteller. The descriptions of Regency London are vivid and create a real sense of time and place. Sam Plank, Martha and Wilson are great characters – well-drawn and totally individual in their creation. The dialogue is believable and the pace well fitted to this genre. The novel shows excellent research and writing ability – a recommended read."
Barbara Goldie, The Kindle Book Review

"Regency police constable Sam Plank, so well established in the first book, continues to develop here, with an interesting back story emerging about his boyhood, which shapes his attitude to crime as an adult. Like the first book, this is not so much a whodunit as a whydunit, and Grossey skilfully unfolds a complex tale of financial crime and corruption. Another feature that really lifts this series for me is the underlying compassion and humanity of the characters, and there are fascinating details about daily life in the criminal world woven into the story, leaving the reader much more knowledgeable without feeling that he's had a history lesson."
Debbie Young, author and book blogger, UK Ambassador for the Alliance of Independent Authors

THE MAN IN
THE CANARY
WAISTCOAT

Susan Grossey

Susan Grossey
Publisher

With grateful thanks to Mr Leonard Wade for the use of the share certificate image on the cover of this book.

This novel is a work of fiction. The events and characters in it, while based on real historical events and characters, are the work of the author's imagination.

Book layout ©2014 BookDesignTemplates.com

The Man in the Canary Waistcoat/ Susan Grossey -- 1st edition
ISBN 978-1-9160019-1-6

For Carol,
who is very fond of Sam but saves her greatest
admiration for Martha

Profit is sweet, even if it comes from deception.

—SOPHOCLES

CHAPTER ONE

All is gone

TUESDAY 19TH APRIL 1825

O ver my years as a police officer, I have seen more corpses than I would care to count. Young and old, rich and poor, lame and sound. Of necessity you become hardened, and you try not to think of the soul that so lately inhabited the body before your eyes. But the ones I can never see without sorrow, without regret for the waste, are the self-murderers, those who choose to end their own life rather than endure whatever despair or shame or fear is tormenting them. The worst of all are the young men: with them, more often than not the police officer has the awful prospect of seeing a young woman crumple before him and disintegrate into a widow at his news.

One such was Henry Dubois, although in the normal run of things I should not have attended him at all. As one of the more experienced constables at Great Marlborough Street, I am rarely called upon in cases of self-murder, where the cause of death is usually clear and the prosecution therefore simple, without the need for further enquiry. And to be honest, once murder by another hand has been ruled out, I prefer not to encourage any investigation; it seems to me barbaric to add to the family's distress with the stain of criminality. But on this damp April morning I was still shaking the rain from my coat and stamping my feet to warm them after the walk to work when Thomas Neale, the office-keeper, called me over.

"Just the man, Sam. Mr Conant needs you to get to an address in Gerrard Street. Looks like self-murder – housemaid came in with a note about an hour ago." He handed me the scrap of paper. "I was going to send young Wilson on his own," he jerked his head to indicate the constable waiting in the corner, hat in hand, "but I had a word with the girl and it sounds like Prussic acid. I don't think he's seen it before, and I'd like someone with him, big lad though he is. Nasty, that is, the first time you see it."

I put my coat back on and tucked the note into my pocket. "Nasty every time you see it, Tom."

Constable William Wilson and I walked briskly through Piccadilly, side-stepping the stall-keepers with their smoking braziers. Glancing down I noticed that Wilson's boots were dull, and I resolved to mention it to him later. Our uniform should always be worn with pride. We both kept a careful eye out for pickpockets who would consider a constable's handkerchief the greatest prize of all, until we turned into Gerrard Street. The house we wanted was on the meaner north side of the street, where the crowded terraces looked across with envy at their grander neighbours. Wilson was usually full of questions, determined to learn and reluctant to show his nerves, but Tom's comment had obviously unsettled him and he hung back as I knocked on the door. A very pale-faced maid appeared, shadows of shock under her eyes.

"Constable Plank and Constable Wilson, from Great Marlborough Street," I said quietly – no point giving any eavesdropping neighbours something else to gossip about.

The maid opened the door and beckoned us in quickly, shutting the door firmly against the chill wind. "The master's in there, well, his body…" she said, pointing to a door off the hallway. "The mistress is with him." We waited. "Did you want me to announce you, only…" A tear made its way down her cheek. The poor girl was obviously terrified of having to look at the corpse again.

"No, no, that won't be necessary," I said, taking off my hat and giving it to her, and indicating to Wilson to do the same – it gave her something to do with her trembling hands.

"Only the master, sir – he, well, he looks…" She bit her lip and looked up at me with more tears standing in the corners of her wide eyes.

I put my hand on her shoulder. "I know: it is very frightening to see, but it will have been quick and painless, and his suffering is over now."

She nodded wordlessly, dropped an untidy curtsey and left us alone in the hallway. I glanced at Wilson, who could now rival the little maid for pallor. "Ready? Try not to show the widow your distress; she has enough of her own." He nodded and I knocked lightly on the door before going in.

Prepared as I was, the stench in the room made me gasp. They had done what they could by leaving the door ajar and opening the window wide behind the drawn curtains, but bitter almonds is a pungent smell that claws at your throat. Wilson clapped his hand to his mouth.

The corpse was laid out on the dining table, covered with a heavy cloth – another attempt, I guessed, at containing the odour. Sitting beside the table, her handkerchief clutched to her nose, was the widow. As she looked up at me, her eyes enormous with grief and fear, I could see that she was no more than thirty.

"Mrs Dubois?" I asked. She nodded. "I am Constable Plank, from Great Marlborough Street. Please accept my condolences. I have been sent to look into the cause of your husband's death, so that the magistrate can decide what needs to be done." She made no movement. "Mrs Dubois, when did you discover that your husband had died?"

She removed the handkerchief and whispered, "About two hours ago, when I finished dressing. He had already come downstairs, to his study, through there, and Emily went to take him a letter and I heard her scream..." She paused to compose herself. "He was already dead; we could tell that straight away. The butcher's lad was in the kitchen, so he helped us carry Henry – my husband – in here. It didn't seem right to leave him on the floor – Henry never did like the cold. That's why I put the blanket over him." She reached out to touch the body, and I stepped quickly across to her. If she lifted that blanket now, what she saw would horrify and haunt her.

"Mrs Dubois," I said, taking her by the elbow and encouraging her to stand, "Constable Wilson and I need to look at your husband's body, to make some notes for the magistrate. I think it best if you go into the parlour and have a warm drink – with the window open, this room has chilled down more than perhaps you realise." I indicated to Wilson to fetch the maid who was waiting in the hallway, and she came to the door, but no further, to coax her mistress away from her vigil. "We will come in to see you in a few minutes." The two women left the room, and I quietly shut the door behind them.

"Your first Prussic acid, isn't it, Wilson?" I asked.

He nodded. "How do you know that's what it is?"

I took from my pocket the note that the maid had delivered from her mistress. "Blue tinge to the face, it says, and a strong smell of almonds."

"More than strong," confirmed Wilson, moving closer to the window.

"Come, Wilson, you'll have to learn to deal with this – it's quite common, with Prussic acid on sale in every chemist's and druggist's shop in the land." He walked reluctantly to my side. "Prepare yourself: it won't be pretty." And I lifted the blanket.

Wilson retched and backed away hurriedly. The corpse's face was bloated beyond recognition; the blue tinge had faded, but the swelling had continued after death, as is common with such poisoning, and the reason why I had not wanted Mrs Dubois to see her husband's body again. The foul smell now filled the room. I took mercy on Wilson, and instructed him to stay by the open window and take down the notes that I dictated to him. "Suspected poisoning by Prussic acid. Male victim, aged about thirty. No other signs of injury. Initial dark colouring now faded, two hours after death. Corpse bloating well advanced, with putrefaction already commenced."

I replaced the blanket over Henry Dubois's face. "The widow said that his study was through there. Come: you can show me what you have learnt about looking for evidence."

Henry Dubois's study was just as expected: solid furniture, an array of books, some papers on the desk. The Turkish rug before the fireplace was bundled up and pushed aside. Wilson followed my gaze.

"I think he died there, on the rug, sir," he said. "Perhaps he was sitting here, in this chair, or standing by the fire," he continued, warming to his theme. "More likely standing. So he drinks the poison – how quickly does Prussic acid take effect?"

"Instantly," I replied. "Muscular spasms first, then suffocation as the lungs stop working."

"So that explains the disorder to the rug – the spasms," said Wilson. "But what happened to the container for the poison?"

"Excellent," I said.

"There was nothing in his hand next door, was there?" Wilson knelt and put his face close to the floor. "Ah!" He reached under the desk. "He must have dropped it as he fell and it rolled here." He stood up and held out a glass phial. The bitter almond smell clung to it still, and I wrapped my hand in a handkerchief before taking it from him.

"Go into the kitchen now," I instructed him sternly, "and wash your hands and under the nails with plenty of soap, in water as hot as you can bear it. Don't put your hands near your mouth until you've done that." Wilson looked petrified, and I took pity on him. "Any drop left won't kill you, but it will make you cast up your account. After that, you can join Mrs Dubois and me in the parlour."

When Wilson returned from the kitchen, his hands bright red from the scrubbing he had given them, Mrs Dubois was just pouring me a cup of tea. I find it best in such situations to give people something familiar and useful to do. She sat back down in a dainty chair and smoothed her skirt before looking expectantly at me.

"I am certain that it was Prussic acid, Mrs Dubois," I said as gently as I could. "The smell of bitter almonds, which you noticed yourself, and other physical signs are unmistakeable. When Constable Wilson and I went into your husband's study, we found a glass phial which we think contained the poison. Here: please look at it, but do not touch it." I took the phial from my pocket, carefully unwrapped the handkerchief, and showed it to her on the flat of my hand. "Did you buy this, or send the maid to buy it? It is sometimes used to treat varicose veins – applied onto the skin, and well-diluted, that is, not swallowed." She shook her head. "Did your husband collect butterflies?"

"Butterflies?" she echoed.

"Such enthusasts often use Prussic acid in their killing jars," I explained.

"No, nothing like that. Henry had little free time – his work at my father's law office kept him very busy. Oh, my father!" Her hand flew to her mouth. "He will be expecting Henry, and wondering what has happened to him. He will be so very angry and ashamed when he finds out."

"Ashamed, Mrs Dubois?" I asked quietly. She nodded, a tear dropping onto the hands clasped in her lap. "Why should he be ashamed of your terrible misfortune?"

"Because it is a sin, constable, to take your own life – a sin, and a crime!" The tears fell more steadily.

"It may be that your husband did not intend to take his own life, that he swallowed the poison in error," I said.

Mrs Dubois shook her head. She reached into her pocket, drew out a crumbled piece of paper and wordlessly handed it to me. I flattened it out and turned it to the light. It seemed to have been torn from a larger sheet of heavy paper, with copperplate writing on its face. I could read "ighting Co Limited", surrounded by elaborate scrolling, and "ertificate" below that. I looked up at Mrs Dubois.

"The other side," she said dully.

The words I read had never been intended for the eyes of a stranger. "My dearest wife, Forgive me for the shame and disgrace that I have brought on you and our son. All is gone, except my love for you both. Forgive me. Henry."

Constable Wilson and I walked back to Great Marlborough Street in silence, each of us preoccupied in our own way with the death of Henry Dubois. In my pocket was his wretched note, which I had borrowed and promised to return. Just as we arrived at the steps leading up to the police office, Wilson stopped.

"Was it painful, do you think, sir? The Prussic acid? Did he feel himself suffocating?"

I needed Wilson's head to be clear, otherwise he would be no use to man nor beast for the rest of the day. And I knew he wouldn't want to show the other constables that he had been frightened by what he had seen, so I turned around and led him to an Irish Ordinary just around the corner. Wilson is a growing lad, with a healthy appetite, so I ordered just a meal for me but a threepenny ordinary for him. He looked surprised when the beer was placed in front of him, as drinking while on duty is frowned upon, but I indicated that he should sup up and he needed no second bidding. I reasoned that the meat and potatoes would soon soak up the beer, and a man needs something stronger than coffee after looking at what Wilson had seen that morning.

We ate in silence, Wilson using a heel of bread to mop the last drops of gravy from his plate. He sat back in his chair.

"So you want to know about Prussic acid?" I asked. He nodded. "The first time I saw it," I started, "I was just the same as you, so there's no shame in that. There would be something wrong with you if you could look on that without horror."

"I expected the colour, but not the swelling. No-one told me about the swelling."

"It's just the body reacting to the poisonous substance. Ignorant people talk of sin leaving the body and so forth, but it's nothing mysterious: it's a purely physical reaction. And the process continues after death, which I didn't want Mrs Dubois to see. Hard enough for us – imagine seeing it when it's someone you care for."

"Would it have hurt?" asked Wilson. "Sometimes you can tell from the face if they died in pain, but with the bloating…"

I shook my head. "I doubt it: it acts so quickly. A druggist I know explained that you need only the smallest amount – two drachms will kill a full-grown man. It has a rather bitter taste, so people tend to mix it with beer or milk – although we found no cup or glass with Dubois, did we, so I assume he just took it plain from the phial. And that's our next task: to find where he bought it, and why. And given that you will be much more to her taste than I will, I suggest that you have a quiet word with that little maid. I doubt a gentleman would run his own errands, particularly to buy something like that."

CHAPTER TWO

Bitter almonds and sweet violets

WEDNESDAY 20TH APRIL 1825

First thing the next morning Wilson beckoned me into the small back room at the police office.

"I spoke to the maid – Emily – like you said, sir, yesterday evening," he whispered urgently. "She was scared at first, as she thought she would be in trouble, but I said that she would not." He stopped and looked enquiringly at me. "I was right, wasn't I, sir? She's not done anything wrong, has she?"

"Well, it depends on what she's done, Wilson, but no, there's no offence in buying Prussic acid, if that's what you're going to tell me."

Wilson took out his notebook, licked his finger and turned over a few pages. "On Friday last, the fifteenth, Mr Dubois called Emily into his study just after breakfast and said that he needed her to buy some items for him. He wrote her a list to show to the druggist, but did not tell her what was on the list."

"The girl cannot read?" I checked.

Wilson shook his head. "Her name, she said, and one or two words from the Bible, but not properly, no."

"So she took the list…" I prompted.

"So she took the list and went directly to Pigeon, Bell and Wheeler in Compton Street – a matter of minutes away from Gerrard Street. Dubois has an account there."

The interior of the druggist's shop was gloomy: dark shelves filled with wooden boxes, ceramic jars and glass bottles formed the side walls, while the narrow space between them was crowded with sacks of tea and spices. The smell was confused and quite overpowering. On hearing the door, a small bald man wearing a large canvas apron that reached the floor despite being turned over several times at the waist came bustling out of the back room.

"Gentlemen," he said, "how may I be of service? A tincture to ward off the spring chill, or some fresh tea for your lovely wives? Some sugar from Jamaica to sweeten their mood?"

"Mr Pigeon?" I asked.

The druggist shook his head mournfully. "Sadly, Mr Pigeon is no longer with us. His name, however, confers much respectability in our little world, and we are proud to retain it on our establishment. My name is Bell."

"Mr Bell, I am Constable Plank, and this is Constable Wilson, both of Great Marlborough Street. We have been tasked by Mr John Conant, magistrate, with looking into the recent death of a local gentleman, Mr Henry Dubois." I was ready to look for a small reaction, but no subtlety of detection was needed: Bell clutched his heart dramatically and staggered back against his counter.

"Mr Dubois!" he repeated. "But a young man only, and in fine health – a cough here, an ache there, but nothing more. And wise enough to turn to his druggist for advice and assistance. May I ask how he did it?"

I ignored the question. "Friday last, the fifteenth, we believe that Mr Dubois sent his maid to you with a list of items for purchase."

The druggist went a little pale. "And you think that..."

I continued. "Do you by any chance remember what was on that list?"

"There is no need for recollection, constable. Mr Dubois is – was – an excellent and regular customer, and as such I was honoured to run an account for him, settled in full every six months." He reached across the counter and pulled a ledger towards him. "Friday last, Friday last – yes, here we go. Epsom salts, three pounds. Peppermint lozenges. Nutmeg and cloves – for a fancy pudding, perhaps. Prussic acid, two drachms." He looked up from the ledger and paused. Then he turned to us. "Prussic acid, two drachms," he repeated tonelessly. "Dear God. He said it was for the veins."

"And how did you supply this acid?" I asked.

"In a small phial of brown glass."

"Like this one?" I took my handkerchief from my pocket and showed the druggist the phial we had retrieved from Dubois's study. Mr Bell nodded.

"Poor devil," he said. "A ghastly way to go." A thought occurred to him. "His wife – did she see him?"

"Only for a moment," I said. "Not later."

"Thank goodness," said the druggist, closing his ledger. "Now, gentlemen, is there nothing I can get for you? Something to soak your aching feet perhaps, after a long day of walking the fine streets of our city?"

Martha looked at the packet I handed her, and then opened it and sniffed. Her smile of delight made me wonder why I didn't spend every last penny I had on making her happy. After all, it was her quickness to smile that had attracted me to her all those years ago – that, and her neat figure, and the unruly curls that refused to stay flat no matter how many pins she used to skewer them. Lucky man that I was, all three were still in evidence.

"To keep in with your linens," I explained. "The druggist said that the violet essence in the papers will make them smell sweet."

Martha came around the table and kissed me on the cheek. "Have you been discussing my linens with all and sundry?" she said, but I could tell she wasn't really cross.

"And he said they would keep the moths away," I added with a wink, and ducked when she took a swipe at me. She sniffed the packet again and then closed it tightly before tucking it into her apron pocket and returning to the stove.

I was just chewing the first mouthful of my dinner when Martha returned to the subject; she rarely forgets anything I say, which is sometimes a blessing and often a curse.

"And what took you to a druggist today?" she asked.

I explained about Mr Dubois. I had no need to tell her the details of his death; perhaps it is ungallant of me, but I had always found it impossible to keep my distress from Martha, and it was no exception when I had first witnessed the effects of Prussic acid, many years ago now. All I had to do was mention the name of the poison, and she could imagine what I had seen. She reached across the table and silently laid her hand on mine.

"For a man to do such a thing, Sam, he must have been truly desperate. Was he married?"

I described his widow and now-fatherless son, and my tender-hearted wife's soft brown eyes filled with tears.

"Have you discovered why he did it?" she asked as she cleared our plates.

"His wife found this," I said, fetching the scrap of paper from my coat and handing it to her. Martha wiped her hands on her apron and took the note from me, turning it to the lamp to see it more clearly. As I had done, she examined both sides of it carefully.

"A certificate of some sort?" she asked. "From a lighting company. Imagine: this is the last piece of paper Mr Dubois looked at. He chose it for his final words to the people he loved the most."

Not for the first time I was brought up short by the clear-sightedness of my practical wife. It was obvious now she said it: this was not just a random piece of paper, but highly significant.

CHAPTER THREE

A faithful and affectionate man

FRIDAY 29TH APRIL 1825

The Dubois maid opened the door and let me in.

"How is your mistress today, Emily?" I asked as I handed her my hat.

She shook her head. "She cries such a lot, sir. At night, so that the boy doesn't hear, but my room is right above hers." She led me to the door of the parlour. "It's a good thing her father lives so close; he calls in most days, on his way home from work." I glanced at the clock on the hall table; it was just before five.

In the parlour, Mrs Dubois was stitching a piece of white linen that contrasted starkly with her black frock;

she tucked it into the workbag at her feet as I entered the room.

"Constable Plank, isn't it?" she asked with the ghost of a smile, and I could see a fleeting glimpse of the lively woman who had captured the heart of a young lawyer, and then disappeared forever with his death. "Has something happened?" She indicated a chair and I sat down.

"Nothing unexpected, Mrs Dubois. As you know, the coroner's jury will meet soon to pass a verdict on your husband's death."

"Where will that be written, constable?"

I was puzzled. "Written, Mrs Dubois? In the court records, you mean?"

She shook her head and looked down at her hands. "I was thinking of the newspapers, constable. Will my husband's death be – reported? Will it be made public that it was…" She turned to me and tears dropped onto her hands. "It's our son, George, you see. I have yet to tell him. He knows his father is dead, of course, but I have let him think that it was accidental. If it appears in the papers that it was not, it will be that much harder to keep it from him."

Not for the first time I wished it were permitted for me to bring Martha with me on these visits. I was at home with logic and order, but when it came to the unexpected and uncertain human heart she was much more expert, and would know exactly what to say to reassure the young woman now looking at me with such anguish.

"None of us can control the newspapers, Mrs Dubois, but I doubt that your husband's death will be of much concern to them." As I said the words I cursed myself for their clumsiness. "I mean that it is not a scandal or connected to anyone famous – such are the shallow appetites of our newspapers. The death of your husband will be of little public interest." The widow seemed to be calmed by my reasoning; she dabbed her tears with a handkerchief and leaned back in her chair. "But I do wonder, madam," I said softly, "whether you should talk more openly to your son, in case he does hear from another quarter. You can imagine that he might be confused by what he hears, or angry to think that you had hidden it from him."

"But how can I tell him something so shocking about his own father?"

"How old is George, Mrs Dubois?" I already knew from asking the maid that the boy was nearly twelve.

"Eleven – no more than a child."

"He is your child, yes, but also well on his way to being a man." I cleared my throat. "Mrs Dubois, forgive me for speaking to you of such things, but I think you are mistaken to keep this from him. He is of an age when things can be explained to him, when he needs things to be explained to him. His father's death will be troubling him. Although you see him as a child, I am sure that he knows only too well that he is now the man of the house. Allow him to start shouldering that responsibility – and you may well find that his strength and understanding will be a comfort to you."

Mrs Dubois twisted her handkerchief in her hands. "But self-murder, constable – a sin!"

I shook my head. "No, madam. A great sadness, yes, but I cannot believe it to be a sin. At the end, your husband was filled with love for you and your son. His final thoughts were of you, not of sin. A merciful God will understand." She looked up at me, and in that small movement I saw the start of hope. "Whatever drove your husband to do what he did, it must have been intolerable. Would it help you if I were to try to find out what it was?"

Mrs Dubois leaned across and grasped one of my hands in both of hers. "Oh, could you, constable? There is nothing I can do now to ease Henry's torment, but if only I could understand his last days – it might stop me wondering and wishing."

I knew what she could not say: wondering whether she could have prevented his death, and wishing that she could have another chance. An image of my life without Martha sprang half-formed into my mind, and the despair I tasted for just a second gave me all the resolve I needed. It would take some squaring with the magistrate, but I was reasonably sure that as long as I fulfilled my regular duties he would turn a blind eye to my spending some time looking into the death of Henry Dubois.

I tried to be as gentle as I could with the young widow, but there was no escaping the fact that I was asking her questions about a man she did not know as well as she had thought. They had been introduced by her brother thirteen years earlier and married soon after. Two years later Henry Dubois had joined his father-in-law's firm. According to Mrs Dubois, her late husband had been a good provider, a hard worker, a caring father and a talented lawyer. Hearing nothing but praise for the recently deceased is normal but unhelpful, so I hardened my heart and continued. Had he any expensive habits? Had his behaviour changed recently, his routine? Did he seem withdrawn or troubled? To all of my questions she gazed at me with sorrowful eyes and shook her head. But there must be something, I was sure: a happily married family man with no money worries and the respect of his peers did not suddenly decide to swig back a phial of Prussic acid.

Just then we heard a knock at the street door. "My father – he has taken to calling in on his way home," said Mrs Dubois, and indeed the resemblance between her and the man who was shown into the room by Emily was unmistakeable.

"Josiah Carley," he said, shaking my hand once he had embraced his daughter.

"This is Constable Plank, papa. We were talking about Henry."

"Indeed?" said Carley, taking the cup of tea that his daughter had poured. "This is surely a simple case, not of much interest to a constable from..."

"Great Marlborough Street, sir, acting on the instructions of John Conant."

He nodded. It gave me no small pleasure to declare that I served such a well-regarded magistrate, when others who held the office, well, you can imagine. "And what precisely is your interest, constable?"

"Constable Plank is of the view that something terrible must have driven Henry to do what he did," said Mrs Dubois quickly, "and I am trying to help him discover what it is. But I am not being much help, am I, constable?"

"It is only a theory, madam," I replied. "Perhaps there was nothing logical that we can discern – perhaps it was a moment of madness or despair that..." I could have bitten out my tongue for suggesting that had Dubois not had such easy access to the Prussic acid the moment might have passed and he could have been alive still. Thankfully the widow seemed not to notice, although the sharp look her father gave me told me that he had followed my thinking. He reached across and patted his daughter on the hand.

"Kitty, my dear, your sister-in-law plagues me daily for those Paris gloves you promised her. Do you think you could fetch them for me?"

Mrs Dubois looked a little surprised, but she put her cup onto the side table and rose to her feet. "Please excuse me, constable – I may be a while as the gloves have been put away for the season."

When Mr Carley and I had sat down again, he spoke to me in urgent tones. "Constable, I want your word that my daughter is to hear nothing of what I am about to tell you." I nodded. "Nothing, do you understand?" I gave my assurance again. He frowned as he tried to find the right words. "Do you have a daughter, constable?" I shook my head. He sighed. "Let me explain, then. A daughter is a lifelong responsibility. You care for her and hold her to you for as long as possible, but one day a man will come to you and ask for her hand. You will look at him and try to see through him, past the fervent promises he is making of fidelity and affection and industriousness, to discern the very core of him. This I did with Henry Dubois. Kitty was besotted with him, and with her dear mother long gone, it was up to me alone to say yea or nay. I asked as many questions as I could, I quizzed him on his past and his plans for the future, and, God forgive me, I believed him." He drained his cup.

"Did he mistreat your daughter, sir?" I asked quietly.

He shook his head. "I almost wish it had been that simple; had she been in distress, I could have separated them and taken her back into my home. But he was faithful and affectionate; she had nothing to complain of."

My pattern-matching mind spotted the two words he had already used. "As for industriousness?" I asked.

"There you have it, constable, there you have it. Dubois was an idle fellow. The despair of his family, I was eventually told by a friend in the Huguenot community, and quite unlike his hardworking relations. When he was courting Kitty, he was receiving an allowance from his widowed mother, but that stopped when he married – conditions of his father's will. And then it became clear that he was singularly unsuited to work of any kind. Position after position was offered, tried and squandered. In desperation I took him into my own firm; there at least I could give him as little work as possible while paying him a living wage."

I looked around me. "But this house, if you'll forgive me, sir – it would cost much more than that."

Carley's shoulders slumped. "That is partly my fault. With Kitty being my only daughter, and looking so like my beloved late wife, I am afraid that I have spoilt her. And when she married, she took her taste for fine things with her. Whenever I could, I would give Dubois a little extra money, saying that as I was the person who had encouraged Kitty to want the best I should help to pay for it, but then one day, about six months ago, he came to me and said that in the future he would manage alone."

"This would be November last year?" I clarified.

"Yes; it was the week of Kitty's birthday, so I remember it."

"And did Mr Dubois explain why he would be able to manage alone?"

"I pressed him, but he was tight-lipped. All he would say was that he had been introduced to a failsafe investment." I looked up from my notebook and Carley raised an eyebrow. "I see that you share my view, constable; if there were such a thing, Fred Robinson himself would mortgage the Palace of Westminster."

I smiled at the thought of our cautious Chancellor making such a rash move. "Was your son-in-law in the habit of making financial investments?" I asked.

Carley shook his head. "He had never spoken of such things before. He was not a chance-taker; he did not frequent the gaming houses or the racetrack."

"And so, for him to be tempted this time, it must have been presented to him as a certainty."

"More than that, constable. Henry was fastidious by nature – he abhorred anything coarse or grubby. He would not have put his money into any underhand or insalubrious enterprise."

I remembered Dubois's neat study, but before we could say anything more the door opened and Mrs Dubois returned, a pair of gloves in her hand. I rose and took my leave, more certain than ever that Dubois's death was no simple matter.

CHAPTER FOUR

Fifteen pounds

MONDAY 2ND MAY 1825

The magistrate John Conant and I were, if not friends, then colleagues with a mutual respect for each other's capabilities. Since the Fauntleroy business a few months before, I like to think that Conant's regard for me had increased — as indeed had mine for him. I admired Conant's diligence in looking beyond the obvious, and his determination to find the truth of a matter rather than the easiest explanation, and I quickly realised that his growing interest in crimes of finance matched my own. Moreover, he was of the view that simply punishing a crime without finding out why it had happened was a wasted opportunity. Like me, he felt sure that if we could understand what drove a man to crime, we would fare much better in deterring him and his fellows from offending again.

I was therefore not surprised when the magistrate sent for me, about a fortnight after the death of Henry Dubois, and asked me to execute a warrant of arrest on a suspected embezzler.

Conant perched his spectacles – a recent acquisition – on the end of his nose and read through the warrant once more before handing it to me and removing the spectacles, rubbing the spot where they had been. He looked tired.

"More financial misdoings, Sam," he said in a tone of regret. "John Dyer, schoolmaster at a charity school. Accused by one of the committee members of embezzling a contribution from a livery company, and putting it to his own service."

"An educated man, then?" I suggested.

"Of twenty years' standing or more," confirmed Conant, shaking his head sadly. He stood and walked to the window of his dining room, pulling the curtain to one side to look down into the street. "Twenty years thrown away for fifteen pounds – not a great recompense, is it, constable?" He turned to look at me and I shook my head.

"Does he know to expect me?" I asked.

"I think not," replied Conant, returning to his seat. "I am acting on the request of the committee, but I understand that they have not apprised Mr Dyer of their suspicion."

"So an ambush, then," I mused as I stood. I could see from the stiffening of his face that I had overstepped.

"A fair arrest of a man on a fair charge, constable," he said sharply, and turned back to his paperwork. Not for the first time I was thankful that my job was simply to apprehend people, and not to weigh the rights and wrongs of their actions.

All Souls' Charity School stood at the corner of Great Titchfield Street and Union Street. Two square columns topped with a triangular pediment gave the front of the building a much grander appearance than the rest of it, which was a square, dirty, brick-built block. Three large arched windows dominated the façade, while a plaque above them reminded all passersby that "This charity school was built in 1791 by the order of the Right Honourable Earl Fitzgibbon, the Very Reverend Robert Winslow DD, Angus Marchman Rector of All Souls', James Handley, George Baker and Francis Edmunds Esquires, Trustees for this Charity". Having attended just such an establishment myself, I could well imagine what was within.

There would be a large schoolroom behind those three windows – sweltering in summer and perishing in winter – where the more promising boys would be taught the basics of reading, writing and numbers, with a view to equipping them for life in an office. Above that would be a much meaner space, where girls would be taught needlework and other skills to put them into service and keep them off the streets. And behind would be the workshops where the less able boys would be given tasks designed to prepare them for jobs as labourers or perhaps craftsmen.

As I stood looking up at the building, a side door banged open and a young curly-haired lad came barrelling round the corner and almost ran into me. Instinctively I grabbed his collar and just as instinctively he started throwing punches in my direction, but as he was no more than six, I was in little danger from his flailing fists.

"Steady, now, lad," I said, trying not to laugh. "What's the rush?"

"Let me go! I ain't done nothing wrong!"

"So why the hurry, and before the bell has rung?" He said nothing but jutted his lower lip at me. "How about if I put you down, and offer you a farthing for some information? Will you stay put?" He nodded. "On your honour?" He nodded again, and I let go of his collar. "Now, do you have a Mr Dyer as one of your schoolmasters?" Another nod. "Can you describe him for me?" I held out a farthing.

The lad grabbed the coin, shoved it inside his jacket, and thought for a moment. "Tall," he said.

"Taller than the other masters, or just taller than you?"

"Taller than all of them," he said.

"Dark or fair hair?"

"Dark."

"Big nose or small one?"

"Smaller than yours." This did not tell me much; after all, my childhood nickname had been Beaky.

"Which way does he walk home when he leaves school?"

The lad shrugged. "The masters leave after us."

"Anything else?" I asked. "I need to know for sure which man is Mr Dyer when he comes out."

"There is one thing, but it'll cost you another farthing," he said slyly. Martha would laugh when I told her that. I felt in my pocket, and nodded. "He limps. Terrible – all lop-sided."

"Well played, lad," I said with a chuckle as I handed over the second coin. "Never give away everything all at once." He grinned at me, stuffed the second farthing down his front to join the first, and scarpered off down the street.

The church bell in the next street chimed five, and as though connected by a hidden wire the school bell rang in echo. The side doors both opened, and from one came a tumble of boys and from the other a more orderly line of girls. Once released they scattered in all directions, and in two minutes the street was quiet again. I waited, and it was not long before the main front door of the school creaked open and a tall, dark-haired man clumped his way down the steps. From his uneven gait, he was unmistakable. I walked swiftly to his side.

"Mr John Dyer?" I asked.

He looked at me wearily. "Aye," he said, "but if you want to enrol the child of some poor unfortunate that you have incarcerated, you will have to apply to the school committee in the usual manner."

"You mistake my errand, sir," I said, and took the warrant from my pocket. "I am Constable Samuel Plank, of Great Marlborough Street, and I have here a warrant for your arrest."

"My arrest? On what charge?" He took the warrant from me and scanned it. "Embezzlement?"

I nodded. "Yes, sir. I am obliged to ask you to accompany me to appear before the magistrate Mr John Conant to answer this charge."

"Now?" Two other schoolmasters came out of the building and looked over at us curiously. Dyer shook his head as if with regret and waved the warrant at them. "Another petition!" he called out.

"Will we see you at the Institute later?" one of them asked in response.

"I doubt it," said Dyer. "Take notes for me, there's a good fellow."

The other man nodded and waved, and the pair walked off. "I was to have attended a lecture this evening at the Mechanics' Institute – I don't suppose...?" Dyer said to me. I shook my head. "But my wife – she will be expecting me."

"We shall send word," I reassured him. "Now, sir, if you would." And we set off in the direction of the police office.

Four of us sat at the table in Mr Conant's dining room above the police office and waited as the manservant lit the lamps to banish the dusk. Dyer seemed less confident than he had, now that he was face to face with the magistrate. To Conant's left was one of his clerks, tasked with taking notes on the evening's proceedings. Once the manservant had left the room, the questioning began.

"Mr Dyer," said Conant, looking at some papers in his hand, "I understand that you have been a schoolmaster at All Souls' Charity School for a good many years." He glanced up at Dyer, who nodded. "And what do your duties entail?"

"I am senior schoolmaster for the upper boys," said Dyer. "Those who show an aptitude for their books are taught first in the lower form, where they acquire the basics of reading and writing, and then at the age of ten they come to me for more advanced tuition – Latin, history, theology of course, some philosophy."

"I see. And does the school ask more of you, perhaps in relation to its raising of contributions?"

Dyer looked uneasy. "That is more properly the responsibility of the committee of superintendence, but we are all encouraged to solicit support where we can."

Conant looked at his papers again, searching for a specific item. "I understand that the chairman of the committee, Mr Josias Greenwood, died recently. In December last year."

"He did," said Dyer solemnly. "A sad loss to all at the school."

Conant looked at him with narrowed eyes – few things irritated the magistrate as much as mock emotion. "Are you sure, Mr Dyer, that you were never engaged in the collection of contributions, perhaps as a favour to Mr Greenwood or another member of the committee?"

"No, sir, never." Dyer's answer came too quickly – he had allowed himself no time to recall any such incident.

"So when Mr William Blades, the treasurer of that committee, says that in mid-March he was indisposed and so asked you to call at the Ironmongers' Company in Fenchurch Street on his behalf to collect an Easter contribution of fifteen pounds, he is mistaken? Or lying?"

Dyer said nothing but he looked quickly around the room as though searching for an escape. I would remember to tell Conant about that reaction; he frequently said that my sharp eyes were an invaluable addition to these interviews. We waited, but Dyer remained silent.

"Mr Dyer, let me tell you what we know," said Conant. "On the morning of Friday the twenty-fifth of March this year Mr Blades gave you a written order to collect a cheque for fifteen pounds from the Ironmongers' Company, excusing you from your teaching duties to perform this service for him. The clerk at the Company, Mr Silas Pallett, received the order later that day from a man he describes as," Conant consulted his notes, "tall and dark, with a limp. In exchange, Mr Pallett handed this tall, dark, limping man a cheque for fifteen pounds, drawn on the banking house of Messrs Freame and Company in Cheapside." He paused again and looked at the schoolmaster, waiting for a response. None was forthcoming. "An entry in that bank's ledger shows that the cheque was presented the following Monday, the twenty-eighth of March, and that fifteen pounds was paid out against it. And yet none of this money has appeared in the school accounts. Can you explain that, Mr Dyer?"

The schoolmaster again said nothing. I leaned forward. "Come, Mr Dyer," I said gently, "it will go better for you if you tell us what happened. Did you perhaps collect the money and then forget to give it to Mr Blades?" He shook his head. "Or were you set upon on your way back from the bank, and the money stolen?" Another shake of the head. I looked up at Conant and shrugged my shoulders – I had offered the schoolmaster two good alibis and he had refused them both.

"Mr Dyer," said the magistrate, gathering his papers into a pile, "if you will not explain yourself to me, then you will have to explain yourself to the court. I am satisfied that there is a case to answer, and the date for your trial at the Old Bailey is set for…" he held out his hand, into which the clerk put a slip of paper, "Wednesday the twenty-second of June, at ten o'clock. As to what to do with you in the meantime…" Mr Conant glared at the schoolmaster over his spectacles. "Embezzlement is a serious offence, Mr Dyer, and I would be perfectly justified in committing you to prison to await your trial. And your unwillingness to speak to me this afternoon makes me wonder whether some weeks in a cell wouldn't make you reconsider."

Dyer's eyes grew large with fear and he gripped the edge of the table. Yet still he said nothing; it was then that I knew that there was something else that frightened him more than the prospect of gaol.

Mr Conant took off his spectacles and wiped a tired hand across his face. "But Constable Plank tells me that you have an invalid wife and several young children at home, and that they would fare very ill without you, which makes it unlikely that you will abscond. You are a schoolmaster, and as such supposedly of good character. Moreover, despite your silence this afternoon, I do not believe that you are an habitual criminal, or that the public at large is in danger from you. And so I am granting you bail. Be under no illusion, Mr Dyer, this is an unusual decision." Judging by the clerk's face, a most unusual one. "In other words, Mr Dyer, you may go home this evening. But if you do not appear at the Old Bailey for your trial at the time and date determined, you will be tracked down and arrested, and matters will go very poorly indeed for you. Do you understand?" The schoolmaster nodded. "Then you may go."

Dyer stood and looked about him, bewildered. I opened the door and he disappeared down the stairs, followed shortly afterwards by the clerk who looked over his shoulder at the magistrate as if to make sure that he hadn't changed his mind. Even I half-expected Conant to cry out, "Stop that man – a mistake has been made!" I made to leave the room myself, but the magistrate called me back.

"Come, Sam, I have further need of you." He waved me into a seat. "No doubt you think I have taken leave of my senses, bailing a man who is plainly guilty." He looked at me questioningly but I simply smiled. It is rarely wise to admit that you think a magistrate is ripe for admission to Bedlam. "John Dyer is no hardened criminal, I think we can agree on that anyway."

"Indeed, sir," I said. "After all, he has worked at the school for over two decades with never a sniff of financial misdoing."

"And now that he knows that we know, he is highly unlikely to embezzle any more money – agreed?"

"Agreed."

"And so he is no danger to anyone, and not going to commit further crimes. What he might do, however, is..."

And then it was clear. "Lead us to whoever is behind all of this," I finished.

Conant nodded with satisfaction. "So you saw it too, Sam? That man is petrified of someone – someone much more terrifying than a mere magistrate."

"I had it in mind myself that Dyer is not the sort of man to concoct a scheme like this alone. Someone else is pulling the strings. And if that person realises that Dyer's embezzlement has been discovered, he might want to make sure that his own involvement remains hidden."

"Which means that he will want to speak to our schoolmaster – and I am relying on you, Sam, to know when that happens." The magistrate stood and held out his hand. "You have all you need?"

"There are plenty of lads happy to keep a watch for a few coins," I confirmed.

Conant suddenly remembered something. "We will need to speak to the banking house, Sam. After all, it is their banknotes that have been stolen. It would be entirely inappropriate for me to go, of course, but I fear that whatever second-rate lawyer Dyer might consult will be too timid or too stupid to think of it. And I know that you have some experience of dealing with bankers."

"I am familiar with the breed, sir," I admitted.

"Then if I may prevail upon you once more, Sam. You noted the name of the house?"

I tapped my forehead to indicate that I had remembered it. "Freame. Cheapside. I shall go first thing tomorrow."

CHAPTER FIVE

Reading by the fire

MONDAY 2ND MAY 1825

"**A** schoolmaster!" Martha was even more outraged than I had anticipated. She banged the teapot down onto the table. "An educated man, in charge of children – children! – and doesn't know the difference between right and wrong."

Despite having been married to a police officer for over twenty years, Martha retained her faith in the essential goodness of people – indeed, I counted on it. On days when I had seen the very worst that someone can do to his fellow man, I comforted myself that an evening by the fireside with my wife would convince me once again that although I moved in a world of shadows, I identified them as shadows only because of the lightness that Martha brought to my life. But her optimism was sorely tested by John Dyer, for, like many without the good fortune to

43

have been educated, Martha held schoolmasters in particularly high regard.

I caught hold of her arm as she bustled across to the range, her outrage bristling from her. "A schoolmaster, yes, my dear, but also a man at the end of his tether, it seems." She effected to check one of the saucepans, but I could tell that she was listening to me. "He has a wife who is ill," I continued, "and six young children – all under seven, and the youngest not three months old."

Martha sat down opposite me. "Mrs Dyer's illness – is it...?"

I shook my head. Martha's own mother had died of childbed fever when Martha was only eight, leaving her father heartbroken – a condition he treated with alcohol until he was no use to man nor beast – and Martha in charge of her five younger siblings. "She has always been delicate, he says, needing tempting with poached eggs and meat broths."

Martha raised an eyebrow. "Poached eggs! I daresay we would all like tempting with those!"

"And a schoolmaster's salary is not overly generous," I continued. "Mr Dyer is paid only thirty-five pounds a year. Far less than me, and I have only a wife to support." Not for want of longing or trying, I added to myself, and I daresay Martha did too. "And a good sturdy wife she is too, with no expensive demands for fancy food." I put my hand over hers to show that I knew what she was thinking.

"Sturdy indeed!" she said, pulling her hand away. "Not the most loving thing a husband can call his wife."

"I've never been one for sugared words, now have I?" I protested. "But to my mind you're the best wife in Marylebone." I winked at her. "Perhaps, at a stretch, in the whole of London. Now, come and sit by the fire and read to me."

When Martha and I were first married, she could read a few words, enough to buy provisions, and write her own name and the numbers. But she saw the pleasure I had from reading stories and she begged me to teach her, saying that she would need to be able to teach our little ones when they arrived. We started out with simple stuff; one of our neighbours was a schoolmaster and he lent us primers that he used with children. Martha was so determined to learn, so disciplined with her practice, that within six months she was reading as if born to it. Now one of our regular habits was for me to borrow a book from Mr Conant (he had a wonderful library, and seemed only too pleased to share his good fortune) and bring it home for Martha to read aloud of an evening. For it turns out that teaching her to read was one of my best decisions: there are few things more comforting to a man than to sit by his own hearth, his wife at his side, listening to her gentle voice carrying him off into other times and other worlds.

"How very apt," said Martha, as she settled into her chair and opened the book at the marker. "It seems that the hero of the next story in this collection is a schoolmaster too. Odd name, though – Ichabod Crane. Is that how you say it?" She showed me the words on the page and I nodded. "Well, I wonder if Mr Crane will steal money from poor children too, like your Mr Dyer." I hoped for John Dyer's sake that the jury would be more lenient than Martha.

CHAPTER SIX

Mr Freame the Quaker

TUESDAY 3RD MAY 1825

The banking house of Freame and Company occupied a slim building near the corner of Cheapside and Milk Street, squeezed between a silk mercer and a trunk maker who both seemed to be busy even at this early hour. Doubtless the Freame banking partners had seen the opportunities for growth as elegant merchants crowded into the area between Millard's East India Warehouse at one end and Dunnetts Toy and Tunbridge Ware Repository at the other. As I looked at the columns and pilasters, at the sparkling windows full of tempting displays being laid out in the shops, I thought how much Martha would enjoy herself here – and how empty my wallet would be at the end of her excursion.

With the clock yet to strike half-past eight, the door to the banking house was still firmly shut, but I knew that at least one clerk would already be inside, busy with his ledgers, and so I knocked loudly. After a few moments I heard the bolt being scraped back and the door opened a few inches. The face of a very young man, still with knees itching from the long trousers as my mother would have said, peered around at me.

"We're not yet open for business," he said tremulously. "Mr Freame says that we cannot let anyone in until nine."

"I am Constable Samuel Plank, here on business for Mr John Conant, magistrate," I explained. "If you tell that to Mr Freame, I am sure he will wish to attend to me before one of your customers arrives and sees me on the premises."

He blinked rapidly and shut the door, then opened it again immediately, said, "Wait here, if you please", and shut it again. Two minutes later he returned, opened the door fully and beckoned me inside, quickly bolting the door shut behind us. He directed me across the banking hall, through a door, a small back office and another door, into what I took to be the parlour given over to the use of the banking partners. Waiting there for me was a man of about my own age. Like me he was a man of economic proportions, perhaps even a little shorter than I am, and dressed in good, plain clothes. He shook my hand warmly, introducing himself.

"Edward Freame," he said, indicating that I should sit. "Delighted to meet you, Constable Plank, was it?" I nodded. "Delighted. May I offer you some refreshment? Tea, perhaps?" He turned to the door. "Stevenson!" he bellowed, and we could both hear footsteps running across the banking hall. "He's only been here a week – doing a favour for his mother, friend of my wife, a widow you know – the friend, not my wife of course!" The young man who had let me in appeared in the parlour. "Tea, I think, if you'd be so kind, Stevenson – two cups this time, one for me and one for our visitor. First brewing, mind you. And have a cup yourself, too." The young man nodded, half-bowed, and scarpered. "Money is tight in that household, I can tell you," continued Freame. "The only place he ever gets first brewing is here. Not sure he'll make a banker, but we do our best to help him – we must always do our best, eh, constable?"

It took me a moment to realise that he was waiting for me to respond. "Indeed we must," I agreed.

"And your business with me today?"

"Yesterday I arrested a man for embezzlement," I began.

"A customer of this house?" asked Freame.

I shook my head. "He's a schoolmaster, at All Souls' Charity School in Marylebone."

"All Souls', All Souls'…" repeated Freame, half to himself. "Not one of ours, I think, although we have several such establishments on our books."

"You provide banking facilities to charity schools?" I said in surprise.

"Oh certainly we do," replied the banker, nodding vigorously. "There is something of God in everybody, and we should each do what we can to help our fellow man. If I can encourage the good work of these schools through my own work, I am happy to be able to do so."

"So Freame and Company is like Barclay, Bevan, Barclay…"

"And Tritton!" finished Freame with glee. "Very like – we are cousins, the Barclays and I. And of the same beliefs, yes: Quakers, every last one of us."

The door was kicked open rather roughly, and in came Stevenson with a tray at a precarious angle. Freame leapt out of his chair and rescued two cups that were sliding to destruction.

"Marvellous, Stevenson – excellent service, if I may say. Should you decide against banking, there will doubtless be a position for you in one of London's finer hotels."

Stevenson blushed with pleasure and backed out of the parlour. Freame winked at me. "A little encouragement can go a long way, constable – and I am sure neither of us is too old to remember being that age, with too many limbs and not enough confidence?" I liked Freame more and more; I looked forward to describing him to Martha that evening, and confounding her expectations of the dour Quaker just as thoroughly as he had confounded mine. But if I had begun to think that he would be an easy man to fool, someone to be taken advantage of in the world of commerce, I was wrong. He sipped his tea, put the cup on a side table, and turned to me with serious eyes. "Embezzlement, you say?" I nodded. "How much?"

"Fifteen pounds."

He shook his head. "No trifling amount, then. And as you are here, I take it that my banking house is implicated?"

I explained about the cheque. Freame leaned back in his chair and yelled down the corridor. "Stevenson! The ledger, if you please – March last!" When the book had been delivered, Freame took it and leafed through to the date in question. "Here we are, here we are: Monday twenty-eighth March, and, yes, a cheque for fifteen pounds was presented to Mr Harris." He looked up at me. "Our senior clerk, so we can instantly dismiss any question of collusion, constable – instantly." I inclined my head in agreement; it was not a matter I had intended to pursue, given what we already knew from Mr Dyer. Freame closed the ledger and clasped his hands over it. "And so, constable?"

"And so, Mr Freame, I will report to Mr Conant that our information is correct – that a cheque for fifteen pounds was presented to your clerk and that money was paid out against it. May I speak to Mr Harris, to see if he remembers the man who presented the cheque?"

"It was more than a month ago, but Harris is a vigilant fellow – he may remember something." Another bellow down the corridor, and this time it was answered by a small, tidy man of about sixty, still in his outdoor coat and clutching his hat in his hand. "Harris, this is a magistrate's constable, hot on the trail of a possible embezzler. The belief is that the criminal – a schoolmaster if you please – brought a cheque to us and obtained fifteen pounds against it."

"To the order of cash?" asked Harris.

"So it would appear from the ledger," said Freame grimly. "We try to advise our customers to take more care, constable, to guard against situations such as this, but perhaps the intention was for the school to use the cash straight away."

"Or maybe everyone involved assumed that a school-master was entirely trustworthy," I suggested.

"Indeed," said the banker crisply. "I have checked the ledger, Harris," he rapped on it with his knuckles, "and it seems that you served the gentleman. Twenty-eighth March last."

"Twenty-eighth March, twenty-eighth March..." said Harris to himself.

"A Monday," added Freame. "First thing in the morning."

Harris frowned in recall, and then his face cleared. "I do remember one fellow," he said, "because he was waiting outside when I arrived – keen as mustard, he must have been, as it was a cold morning to be standing around. Yes, I do believe he mentioned that he was connected with a school – one of the charity schools, I think. I daresay he was in a rush to get to his lessons."

I looked up from the notes I was making in my book. "Can you remember anything about his appearance?" I asked.

Harris paused to think back. "Tall – but then everyone seems tall to me! Thin, and not at all robust. I did wonder if he was an old soldier, with that limp. Lucky to get work, with so many back from the wars."

"Is that what you need, constable?" asked Freame. I nodded. "Thank you, Harris," he said, turning to his clerk. "You have been your usual thorough self. Stevenson has made tea, if you're feeling brave." Harris smiled and left. "It was the limp that confirmed it for you, wasn't it?" said the banker. I had been right: not much escaped him.

"I think he's our man," I agreed.

"Not looking good for the poor fellow, is it?" asked Freame.

I wondered whether he knew quite how bleak the situation was. I shook my head. "The courts take a very dim view of embezzlement," I confirmed. "Theft from an employer, with all the breach of trust that that entails." I waited to see if the banker would say anything but he remained silent. "It's the scaffold, Mr Freame."

"The scaffold!" He jumped to his feet in agitation. "The scaffold, for a desperate cripple trying to feed his family – sheer barbarism. It cannot be permitted, constable – I will not allow it. The banking house cannot allow it." He walked across to a bookshelf and started scanning it, before reaching for a folder and pulling it out. He leafed through some papers and handed me a pamphlet. "Here: have you read this?"

I took it from him. "Blood for Gold, or Death for Forgery proved to be Inexpedient, Unjust and Unscriptural" said the bold lettered title, and beneath it was a phrase that made me shiver: "Suggested by the Recent Case of Mr Fauntleroy". I looked up at the banker.

"No need to read it all," he said, "but I have indicated the key passages – take a look at those." And he busied himself with a newspaper while I read. There were several sentences that the banker had marked with lines in the margin, but one in particular caught my eye as he had also underlined it with heavy black ink. I read it aloud: "Mercenary indeed must be the wretch, who would demand the life of any man as an imaginary compensation for the loss of a little gold." Freame put down his newspaper and looked at me.

"But surely," I asked, "a banker is expected to be mercenary."

He smiled sadly. "Check your dictionary, constable. Materialistic, perhaps, or mercantile, or even acquisitive on behalf of his customers. But never mercenary, for that requires the putting aside of morality and human decency." He stood and took the pamphlet from me. "And for that reason we must find a way to punish this poor man to the satisfaction of the courts, but without resorting to the noose. Should it come to it, I shall refuse to press charges, and the bank will pay over the missing fifteen pounds to the school. Please convey my respectful regards to the magistrate, but I rely on you to make my position quite plain to him."

Conant sighed as he listened to me later that day. "Mr Freame is not the first Quaker banker who has taken such a stance," he said, "and I am sure he will not be the last until this whole wretched business is resolved. You know as well as I the endless debate around the use of the scaffold." He stood and walked across the room, to stand at the window gazing down into the street. I waited; there are few things more irritating and less productive than to interrupt a man who is deep in thought. After a few minutes the magistrate turned and looked at me. "We must both apply ourselves to this situation, constable – you with your particular skills and me with mine. I would like you to find out more about Mr Dyer. Speak to his fellow schoolmasters, perhaps, and his wife. Speak to the man himself if you think you can get more out of him than I managed. Meanwhile I will raise the matter with some lawyer friends of mine – I know several who are in sympathy with Mr Freame's view. Between us, we should be able to find a way to levy a more proportionate punishment, do you not think?"

I stood and put my hat on. "I do, sir, most assuredly. Something must have made a man of hitherto unblemished reputation take such a step. If we can find what that is, and fortune favours us with a tender-hearted jury, we may be able to save the schoolmaster from the scaffold."

"And in the meantime, constable..." he looked at me questioningly.

"And in the meantime, sir, I will endeavour to find out who or what has frightened Mr Dyer into silence."

CHAPTER SEVEN

Non compos mentis

THURSDAY 5TH MAY 1825

But before I could make much progress with Mr Dyer and his embezzlement, my attention was drawn back to another matter. The verdict of the coroner's jury was as I had hoped, but the relief I felt as I left the court told me that I had allowed myself to become more embroiled in the Dubois situation than I had realised. I turned up Ludgate Hill and made my way directly to the law offices of Josiah Carley. The size of the premises was neither mean nor extensive, indicating a solid firm of good standing.

The young man who answered my knock was wearing a coat clearly inherited from someone much larger; it hung from his shoulders, and he repeatedly and pointlessly pushed back the cuffs. The ink smudges on his fingers told me that he was a junior clerk, and his relegation to door duties told me that he was not much good at it. He led me into a waiting parlour, relieved me of my hat, and a minute later returned to show me into Carley's room.

"You have come from the coroner's court?" asked Carley once we were alone.

My assumption had been correct; Dubois's father-in-law had known only too well what was being decided that morning and had been waiting anxiously for the verdict.

"I have indeed, sir," I said.

"And?"

"Temporary insanity," I confirmed.

Carley passed a hand across his forehead. "Not felo de se?" I shook my head. "Thank God."

I took my notebook from my pocket and turned to the words I had written that morning. "If I may?" I asked. Carley nodded and I read aloud, "Henry George Louis Dubois, on the nineteenth of April 1825, committed suicide. He was afterwards found, by inquisition of the coroner, to be non compos mentis.' After the verdict I spoke to the coroner's clerk, and he showed me a letter, from you, sir, confirming that Mr Dubois's mind was much troubled, that he had spoken to you of nightmares and visions, and of how he would walk for hours at night, too terrified to take to his bed. And yet his widow made no mention of this peculiar behaviour when I spoke to her."

Carley pushed himself up with a grunt and strode to the window. After gazing out for a few moments, he turned to me.

"What would you have done in my place, constable? The law concerning suicide is pitiless: a verdict of felo de se makes a man a felon, condemns him to a shameful burial, and forfeits all of his property to the Crown. It takes no heed of the circumstances – either of the poor devil who is driven to such an act, or of those he leaves behind. Non compos mentis at least allows my daughter and grandson to keep their home. As a lawyer, it pained me to write that nonsensical – that untruthful – letter, but as a father, what else could I do?" He sat down behind his desk and looked at me with haunted eyes. "Will you have to tell the coroner what you know, constable – about the letter?"

I closed my notebook. "I have no record of any letter, sir. I suggest that you visit your daughter as soon as you can to put her mind at rest concerning the court's verdict."

Carley nodded wordlessly, then dropped his head into his hands. I left him to his thoughts; very little is more devastating to a man than to discover that the code by which he has lived his life cannot, after all, be relied upon.

As I left Carley's office, the clerk drowning in his own coat hurried over to see me off the premises. He clutched my hat in his hands, and seemed reluctant to let it go.

"A sad business for you all," I said, to give him an opening. "I understand that Mr Dubois was a popular man."

The clerk nodded vigorously. "Aye, always ready with a smile, and not what you might call a taskmaster, neither. Not like..." He stopped suddenly and glanced over his shoulder. "Oh, sir, you won't tell what I just said, will you?"

"How about this, my lad," I said. "I won't tell him that, if you tell me something else." The clerk looked nervously at me, checked again over his shoulder, and nodded. "Did Mr Dubois act strangely in the last weeks of his life?" No reply. "Did he say or do anything unusual?" Again, nothing. "Did he meet anyone new?" Bullseye: the clerk's eyes widened. "Who did he meet? A lady who was not his wife?"

"Oh no, sir, nothing like that. It was a man – but not a gentleman, and not here in the office. They met, oh, at least twice I saw them, round the corner in the churchyard. I can't be sure what, but I saw Mr Dubois give the other fellow something – some paper, I think."

"Can you describe this other man?"

The clerk thought for a moment. "Tall, a bit shabby. An old soldier, I thought perhaps, down on his luck."

"Why an old soldier?" I asked casually as I put on the hat that the clerk had finally handed over.

"He looked like he'd been wounded – terrible limp he had."

CHAPTER EIGHT

The delicate wife

MONDAY 16TH MAY 1825

I am not a religious man. I know many men say it, often with a note of pride in their voice, as though they know some secret of the universe denied the rest of us. But I mean simply that I have little time for the manmade rules and orders that are treated as though they come from God. That there is a God, of this I am certain – but I doubt that He would choose to communicate His will through that flock of cawing crows who call themselves His ministers. Rather, I believe that He appears in the eyes of a young mother gazing at her baby, and in the gentle hands of an old woman wiping the brow of her dying husband, and in the generosity of friends who share their last piece of bread when starvation beckons.

For myself, I find that God is silent when we are supposed to hear Him, during Sunday services, and so I usually find an excuse not to attend. Martha is used to my ways now, and we no longer quarrel on this matter. But often, as I walk around this great, filthy, threatening, promising, thriving city, I see His work. And sometimes, as on this day, He draws me into His buildings to sit quietly for a while and listen to His counsel.

All Souls' in Langham Place is one of the new marvels of Marylebone. Its graceful portico columns and elegant spire soar to the heavens, and inside Nash has forsaken the fancy embellishments found in so many other churches to create an airy space that I find liberating. Some have criticised the scantiness of his decoration, even comparing the building to a warehouse, but I find it uplifting: without distractions and impediments, my mind can wander free, and whenever I pass I try to call in for a few minutes' reflection.

Of course on this occasion it was not a chance visit; ever mindful of Mr Conant's intentions in granting bail to the schoolmaster, whenever possible I made sure that I was in the vicinity of Dyer's school at the end of the day. On every day so far he had simply turned his step to home, but today he went westwards instead, and I followed. He turned into Langham Place, reached the corner of Riding House Lane and stopped, looking around furtively. I quickly mounted the church steps in order to

stand behind one of the columns and so observe him un-
seen. The bells above us started to toll the hour, and just
then another man stepped out of the shadows and approached Dyer. I shuffled slightly round the column so
that I could see both men.

Dyer's companion was unmistakably a flash man; his
careful checking of his surroundings marked him out to
me as someone who was used to being watched. His fair
hair was cut fashionably, and his clothes – from the bright
yellow waistcoat to the artfully arranged cravat – suggested someone with altogether too close an acquaintance
with his tailor and his looking glass. What was a charity
schoolmaster doing associating with such a swell?

Even with my obstructed view, I could tell that Dyer
was frightened of this man; his shoulders were down, and
although he was taller than his companion, he did his best
to appear shorter. I could hear nothing of their words,
but once the tolling of the bell had stopped, I could discern the tone, which was that of a disagreement. The
swell held out his hand, waiting to be given something,
and the schoolmaster clasped his own hands to his chest
and then opened them to show that they were empty.
The swell pushed his face close to Dyer, said something
more, and then strode off. I saw the schoolmaster put one
hand to his heart, and use the other to prop himself
against a wall.

I gave him a moment to gather himself, before walking down the steps and past him, and then stopping as though I had suddenly caught sight of him.

"Why, Mr Dyer, isn't it?" He looked at me and blinked rapidly. "Constable Plank," I explained, "constable to Mr Conant." Still he said nothing. "Taking an evening stroll?"

He finally found his tongue. "Ah yes, constable – I recognise you now. No, well, yes, that's it: an evening stroll. After a day of rowdy boys, I need a few minutes to myself." As he spoke, he craned to see past me.

"Are you looking for the man in the canary waistcoat?" I asked.

He stared at me. "So you…"

I nodded. "And I know that he is no schoolmaster, Mr Dyer." I waited: leave a silence for long enough and no man can resist filling it.

"No, indeed. He is more of, well, an adviser."

"And on what does he advise you, Mr Dyer?"

The schoolmaster's eyes darted from side to side as he groped for an answer. "On schemes for making money."

"Speculation?" I asked in surprise.

"Oh no, not speculation – investment. Investment in opportunities that need a little time to mature."

"And what was the purpose of today's meeting – for your adviser to hand over some of your profits?"

"Well, no," said Dyer quietly. "He had heard of another scheme and wondered if I would like to invest further, but it is not possible this month."

"Mr Dyer," I laid a hand on his arm, "listen to me. I have dealt with many men in canary waistcoats, and I know how they run their business. And today he was not suggesting: he was demanding. What was he demanding, Mr Dyer?"

The schoolmaster looked straight at me for the first time, and in his eyes I saw a look I know well: that of a man who is trapped and can see no way out. He shook his head tightly, turned from me and hurried off down Riding House Lane, back towards his school.

"Some broth, that walnut loaf I made this afternoon, pass me four of those apples, Sam – no, not the bruised one, I'll put that in a pie tomorrow." Martha had listened to my description of my meeting with Dyer, and now she was moving purposefully around the kitchen, filling a basket as she went. The walnut loaf was a particular favourite of mine and I was sorry to see it go. She caught sight of me sitting bemused at the table, and rolled her eyes. "Good heavens, Sam – after all these years! Surely you know by now that if you want to find out what is troubling a man, you speak to his wife. You have Mr Dyer's address?" I nodded. "His wife is delicate, and has six little children. A basket of nourishing items will get me into the parlour, and a sympathetic ear will do the rest."

"Should I come with you?"

She snorted. "A great police officer sitting in the corner of the room scribbling in his notebook is hardly going to encourage confidences, is it now, Sam? You get on with polishing those boots, and I'll be back later. You can heat that stew if you're peckish."

I was just wondering whether to tackle the stew after all, when Martha arrived home. She handed me her empty basket and unpinned her bonnet. In the kitchen, she lifted the cover on the pot of stew, tutted, and put it on the range. I went up behind her and put my hands on her waist.

"It's not that I don't know how to heat it, Mar," I said. "I just don't like to eat without you, you know that." She tutted again, but her heart wasn't in it.

When the stew was warm, she served and we sat at the table. After a few reviving mouthfuls, she was ready to talk.

"Eight of them, Sam, in three rooms smaller than ours. She does her best, I can tell, but she's not a robust woman, and no mother nearby to help. They moved up from Portsmouth, she said, when he was looking for work. She thought at first that I was one of those do-gooders looking for souls to save, but when I explained who you were and why we were concerned, well, it was like taking the cork out of a bottle and she couldn't stop talking. Seems her husband's one of those men who like to tell their wives everything but then won't listen to any advice," she looked up at me and I put on my most innocent face, "which means that the poor woman has all of the worry without being able to do anything about it."

"And what has her husband been telling her recently?" I asked as I leaned over to help myself to more stew from the pot.

"Well, you were right to think that it was something to do with speculation, Sam. She didn't call it that, of course – 'investment opportunities', she said, just like him – but in short he has been persuaded to put his money into some sort of scheme to set up a new company. And of course the Dyers have yet to see any money back from the scheme."

"Is he being pressured to put in more money? The swell I saw him with seemed to be asking for something."

Martha shook her head. "No: he's told them that there is no more money. But they do want something more from him." She put down her spoon. "Apparently they have told Dyer that if he wants his money back, now he has to help them find more people to invest in the scheme. Every week he has to meet someone – your man in the bright waistcoat, I imagine – and hand over a list of people he has subscribed to the scheme."

It certainly made sense. "A schoolmaster would be seen as a respectable fellow," I mused aloud, "and he meets plenty of people." And then a thought occurred to me. "But if he can't find enough subscribers to satisfy them..."

Martha nodded grimly. "Sarah – Mrs Dyer, that is – says that he tried to buy himself out of the scheme, but they wouldn't let him."

"That might explain the embezzlement."

"Almost certainly – the timing is right. Just after Easter, Sarah said, he came home in a better mood than she had seen for months, wearing a new pair of trousers and laden down with food and treats for the children. He said that his investment had come right, but a few days later he was even more miserable than before."

A thought occurred to me. "Did Mrs Dyer mention how her husband came to be involved in the scheme in the first place?"

Martha smiled at me. "I haven't been married to a constable for all these years for nothing, Samuel. I thought you might want to know that. It seems that Mr Dyer sups regularly at the Turk's Head in Broad Street, and someone approached him there." She stood and cleared the table. "Now, where did I put that other walnut loaf?" I had to laugh: she knew full well that had she mentioned the loaf earlier, she would have come home to nothing more than crumbs and an empty plate.

CHAPTER NINE

The candle in the cellar

TUESDAY 24TH MAY 1825

The courtroom was crowded and I had to elbow my way in, murmuring "Police officer, police officer on duty" when I thought it might do me some good. I edged my way on to a bench, and once I had apologised to my neighbour for my proximity and removed my hat and placed it on my knee, I looked down into the well of the court. Standing by the far door, with three other men who looked from their dress to be fellow constables, was Wilson.

It was thanks to him that I was in court at all. The previous day he had caught up with me as I was leaving Great Marlborough Street and had walked home with me, explaining that he was to give evidence in an arson trial and that, as it was his first appearance at the Old Bailey, he wanted to check the procedure. Big as he is, the poor lad was pale with nerves and kept gnawing at his lip, asking the same questions over and over again and making messy notes in his book. He was still by my side when I arrived home, where my soft-hearted wife took one look at his pasty face and all but dragged him indoors for a hearty slab of pie, with extra potatoes and gravy. What with Wilson's worries and Martha's none-too-gentle digs in the ribs, I found myself promising that I would come to court so that he would have a friendly face to look at. I now stared across at him until he felt my eyes on him, and we nodded at each other.

As it happens, I could remember the day of the fire very well, for I had been in the office when Wilson had arrived. The fire had taken hold in the early hours of the morning on a Wednesday in April, and Wilson had happened upon it while making his way to work. As he told it to me, he had managed to discharge his duty at the scene – checking for anyone trapped inside and then assisting the man from the fire office in looking for the cause of the blaze – but afterwards he started to shake and by the time he made his way to Great Marlborough Street, he was in something of a state. I sent a lad to buy a tankard of ale from down the road, and watched as Wilson drank it. His face was smudged with soot, his hair likewise smeared, and the smell of charcoal swirled around him. I knew from experience that he would be tasting the fire for days, but what I did not know until he told me that morning was that two of Wilson's young siblings had died in a fire the previous year. An unattended grate, a moment's distraction – the story was all too familiar. I had put a hand on Wilson's shoulder, and made no comment as he cried quietly.

I looked over at the bench to see who was presiding, and was pleased to spy Sir John Bayley. With his quiet voice and sympathetic manner, he would give Wilson a much more gentle introduction to the trial process than many I could mention. I remember attending one of his trials where his good temper had been so obvious – and so rare in the Old Bailey – that a French advocate had remarked loudly to his clerk that "il s'amuse à juger", and I honestly believe that he did.

We were the third case of the day, so the jury was already sworn in and getting into their stride as the clerk stood, turned to look at the man in the dock, and read in a bored monotone from the papers in his hand.

"Edward Wakefield, you stand indicted that on the sixth of April last you feloniously, wickedly and unlawfully did set fire to a certain house then being in your possession, with intention to defraud the London Assurance Company for houses and the loss of goods from fire. You also stand indicted that you did attempt to defraud Mr Joseph Williams." The clerk looked up from his papers at the defendant. "Edward Wakefield, how say you? Are you guilty or not guilty of the said felony?"

In the dock was a man of about fifty, his face shining red from scrubbing and shame, his hands white-knuckled as he clutched the wooden bar. He stared at the judge for a few long seconds before that kindly man leaned forward and said, "You must answer the clerk, Mr Wakefield. You must tell him whether you are guilty or no, so that we may all proceed with our business."

"Not guilty, sir," said Wakefield, and the clerk noted the plea on his papers.

The trial started. A young lawyer whom I did not recognise rose to his feet and called his first witness.

"Who is the lawyer?" I asked my neighbour.

"Kerr," he said. "Started at the Bailey this week. Full of his own importance, so should do well here."

"Mr Granger," began Kerr, "Mr Granger, you keep a public house in Bird Street in Piccadilly."

Granger – showing the unmistakable signs of his trade with his mottled cheeks, generous girth and strong hands – nodded. "Yes, next door to that man."

"Mr Wakefield – the prisoner in the dock?" Granger nodded again. "And what sort of premises does Mr Wakefield keep there?"

"It is an eating house, sir."

"And can you remember what happened in the early hours of the sixth of April this year?"

"I was abed with my wife, when we heard shouting in the street. I put my head out, and a woman was calling to the watchman that there was a fire at Mr Wakefield's shop. So I told my wife to alarm our lodgers – we have two – and the servants, and then I ran out into James Street to try and help."

"James Street?"

"Wakefield's premises – like mine – has a front entrance in Bird Street and a back door in James Street. I tried to force Wakefield's door but it was barred. I hammered on it and then ran round to the front, crying 'Fire!' and 'Watch!' to get help. I went to Wakefield's front door and was able to force it open with my shoulder, but as soon as I got inside I could see that the stairs were ablaze. A watchman came running up behind me and sprang his rattle, which brought out the rest of the neighbours. Mr Stenning from two doors along came in with his axe and started breaking down the burning stairs."

"And why did he do that?" asked the lawyer.

Granger looked as him as though he were mad. "To stop the fire spreading, of course. We could tell that the fire had started down below, and we wanted to stop it taking hold above. It is what any sensible man would have done."

The lawyer coloured as a few ladies in the court tittered at this put-down. "And did you see Mr Wakefield?"

"He was not there, no – not for another quarter of an hour."

"But surely you were making something of a racket, breaking down his door and his stairs?" The lawyer was doing his best to win back his audience with a little humour.

"Indeed, sir: we were making as much noise as we could, to rouse anyone in the premises. I called out for Mr Wakefield and for his wife and servant, to tell them of the danger."

"And yet he did not appear for a quarter of an hour?"

"No, and when he did appear in the street, he wanted more than anything to go into the cellar. He was most agitated."

I looked across at Wilson, and was gratified to see that he had his notebook in his hand and was paying careful attention. On my first appearance as a witness at the Old Bailey I had failed to remember a point made earlier in the trial, and the look of disdain I had received from the judge was not something I wished to visit on another constable, and so I had schooled Wilson to listen to every word that was said.

"Did Mr Wakefield go down into the cellar?" continued the lawyer.

"No: the watchman and I held his arms and stopped him."

Kerr nodded and made a note on his papers. He leafed through a couple of sheets and turned back to Granger.

"How long have you lived in Bird Street?"

Granger looked thoughtful. "Just over five years. Perhaps five years and two months."

"And was Mr Wakefield already in residence when you moved in?"

Granger shook his head. "No: he moved in only six months ago, in September last I think."

The lawyer looked again at his notes, but finally had to admit that he had run out of questions. He motioned to the clerk, who beckoned Granger from the stand and called the next witness in his place. William Crawford was a small, quietly-spoken man, neat in his movements, and I noted that he paused after each question, giving himself time to think. As a result, his answers were precise and specific, which is a trait I much admire in a person. Too many people hurry and bluster, when a moment's thought would benefit both them and their listeners.

"Mr Crawford," asked Kerr, "where do you live?"

"My family and I live at number 7 Bird Street, next door to Mr Wakefield."

"And on the morning of the sixth of April this year, were you alarmed?"

"Yes: there was knocking at my door and a cry of fire."

"A cry of fire?" queried Kerr.

"Someone shouted, 'Get up or you will be burnt!'. And so I immediately went up and fetched two of my children downstairs, calling my wife to get the baby. We all went out into the street."

"Is there a pump in the street?" asked Kerr.

"Yes: there is one close to Mr Wakefield's house. I saw the watchman and two men – whom I now know to be Mr Granger and Mr Stenning – breaking in the glass at the front of Mr Wakefield's premises, and my elder boy and I took buckets to the pump and fetched water to throw on the fire."

"At any point did you go into the cellar of the prisoner's house?" asked Kerr.

"Mr Granger, Mr Stenning and the watchman went first, and I followed halfway down, but I did not go into the cellar."

"Could you see anything unusual in the cellar, from your vantage point on the stairs?"

A slightly longer pause. "We have been told that there was a candle, but I did not see it myself."

"And what happened next, Mr Crawford?"

"I turned to go back up the cellar stairs, and saw Mr Wakefield waiting at the top of the stairs."

"Was he intending to go into the cellar?"

"A man's intentions are his own, sir," said Crawford. "I would not presume to guess."

Kerr frowned and pursed his lips. "Would you presume to describe his clothes for us, Mr Crawford?"

"Certainly. He was completely dressed."

"Dressed? In his day clothes?"

Crawford nodded. "A drab jacket, yes, and worsted stockings. He had his apron in his hand, and wore no hat, but otherwise he was dressed as usual."

"And you, Mr Crawford – what were you wearing?"

"A nightshirt, with a coat thrown over."

"Because you had been woken from sleep. Which suggests that Mr Wakefield had been awake already, before the fire, before the alarm, before everything." Kerr paused; Crawford made no response. The judge cleared his throat meaningfully, and the young lawyer hurried on. "Did you know Mr Wakefield?"

"Our wives spoke regularly, about children and suchlike, I believe."

"He was a married man, then?"

"He was."

"And was his wife at home on the night when the fire broke out?"

"She was not, no. She had told my wife that she was visiting her sick mother, in Bow I believe, and she was from home on the night of the fire, thank goodness."

"A timely coincidence, one might say," mused the lawyer as though to himself. "Thank you, Mr Crawford."

The next to be called was a rotund little body called Bertha Davis, whose hands were never a moment still but played along the wooden rail in front of her or fiddled with her cap or, lacking other amusement, turned over each other. She gazed about her, and when her eyes lighted on the judge sitting high above her, his wig upon his head, they widened in astonishment. When the lawyer asked a question she would glance quickly at him, but the judge fascinated her and she could barely tear her eyes from him.

"Miss Davis," said the lawyer, his voice rising to catch her attention. "Miss Davis, are you servant to the prisoner?" Little Bertha looked pleadingly at the judge.

"The prisoner, madam, is Mr Wakefield," explained Sir John in a kindly tone. "What we wish to know is, do you work for Mr Wakefield the eating house keeper?"

The woman nodded several times and spoke directly to the judge. "Oh yes, sir. I do, sir. Yes, his servant, sir. Indeed, sir, yes. Been with him and Mrs Wakefield about seven months on the night of the fire. I remember it was seven months because it was my brother's birthday on the day I started with them."

Sir John nodded and then indicated with his hand towards Kerr. "There we go now, madam. Quite simple, is it not? This gentleman has a few more questions for you, I feel sure." He smiled encouragingly.

Kerr blinked a few times; young lawyers are often surprised to discover that some judges pay very close attention to proceedings in court. "On the night of the fire," he finally said to Bertha, "at what time did you go to bed?"

Bertha kept her eyes fixed on the judge. "At about half past eleven, sir. I had just heard the church strike."

"And did your master go to bed at the same time?"

"Yes, sir."

"But your mistress was from home that night?"

"Yes, sir. Her poor mother was sick with the rheumatics."

"During the time that you had lived at your master's house, had your mistress ever slept out?"

Bertha thought carefully before answering. "No, sir," she answered with surprise. "Not once."

Kerr looked meaningfully at the jury and repeated, "Not once." He glanced down at his notes. "How did you know about the fire?" he asked Bertha.

"There was a knocking at my door. I opened it and saw my master there. He said that we were afire and I should get out."

"And how was he dressed?"

"In his clothes for work – the same clothes he wore during the day."

"And was he carrying anything?"

This caught my attention. I looked across at Wakefield; from what Wilson had told me the previous day I already knew much of what the servant Bertha had told us, but this was something new, and I have found that it is useful to watch a prisoner at such times. Wakefield's shoulders fell and he shut his eyes. So he had been carrying something.

"He had his till under his arm," confirmed the servant.

"That is the box for the takings from his eating house?" asked Kerr. Bertha nodded. "Thank you, Miss Davis, that is all."

Bertha stayed where she was, her eyes as ever fixed on the judge. After a few moments, Sir John leaned forward. "You may go now, madam. You may leave the court." The servant curtseyed and tried to back out of the dock; titters from the public gallery were quickly silenced by a stern frown from the judge.

It was now the turn of young Wilson to take the stand. He made his way across the courtroom, squeezing his large frame between the crowds of people. Once in the dock, he bowed to the bench, as I had reminded him, then stood upright, as though on parade, to face his fate.

"Constable Wilson," began Kerr in a companionable tone, "I believe that you were the first officer to arrive at the scene of the fire."

"Yes, sir, although I had not been sent there. I was on my way to work when I heard the alarm and thought I might be of some assistance."

"And did you speak to Mr Wakefield when you arrived?"

"Yes, sir, I did. He was standing in the street, fully dressed as has been said, and I asked him if there was anyone inside the house. He said that his wife was from home, and that the servant – Miss Davis – was out of doors."

"The servant has said that her master was carrying his till – did you see this?"

Wilson shook his head. "He did not have it when I spoke to him, but later, when I was checking the premises, I found it hidden in the yard, in a sack under a barrel."

"Hidden, you say? Not simply dropped, or stored for security?"

"In my opinion it was hidden, yes, sir."

"Did you venture into the cellar of the eating house, constable?"

"Once the fire was dampened, and in the company of a fireman who had now arrived, I did go into the cellar, yes, sir."

"And what did you see there, constable?"

"I saw heavily charred beams, which I took to indicate the point at which the fire started. When the fireman and I looked more closely, he pointed something out to me and I observed a candle burning in the joists. There were three candles in all, but two had gone out. I picked up what one of the candles had been standing on – I have it here." He reached into his pocket. "There was this piece of coal, with a potato standing on it. There is a hole, here, in the potato where the candle was placed. This candle had gone out, but you can see the tallow on the potato and the coal – and the floor around it was all scorched."

"What did this arrangement suggest to you, constable?"

Wilson looked across at me, and I nodded at him. I could understand his reluctance; what he said next could speed a man to the scaffold. But a police officer is bound by oath and character to tell the truth at all times, and Wilson was learning that this is a heavy responsibility. He turned back to the bench and looked up at the judge, whose eyes were fixed on him. "It suggested to me, sir, that the fire had been started deliberately."

"Thank you, constable," said Kerr with the air of a conjurer successfully completing a difficult trick. "That will be all."

Wilson bowed again to the bench and returned to the company of his fellow constables. I was pleased to see some colour return to his face now that his ordeal was over.

The final witness was John Bickerstaffe, a clerk at the London Assurance Company. Kerr handed him a piece of paper, and the clerk inspected it carefully.

"Please could you explain to the court what that paper is," instructed the lawyer.

"It is a receipt for payment of a premium to our company," said Bickerstaffe.

"Is that your corporation seal on the receipt?"

The clerk peered closely at the seal, turning it to the light to make certain of it. "It is, yes."

"And does the receipt correspond?" asked the lawyer.

Bickerstaffe turned to a ledger at his side, opened it to a marked page, and looked once again at the receipt. "Yes: here it is in our books. This receipt was issued on the eleventh of December, 1824."

"And it is in the name of the prisoner, and specifies his address?"

"Mr Edward Wakefield, number 9 Bird Street in Piccadilly," confirmed the clerk.

"Is the prisoner shown as the owner of the premises?"

Bickerstaffe again consulted his ledger. "No; he is the tenant. Number 9 and number 11 are owned by Mr Joseph Williams."

Bickerstaffe was dismissed. Kerr bowed to the bench, indicating that his witnesses were at an end. He gathered his papers into a pile and turned to the bench.

"My lord, and gentlemen of the jury," he began, "what we have here is a clear case of arson. The prisoner took out insurance with the sole aim of claiming on it, and paid only a single premium. He then made sure that his wife was from home – for the first time in six months – and set the fire himself, by fixing and lighting candles in the basement. He woke the servant to save her, but she noted that he himself was already fully clothed, despite the early hour, which shows that the fire did not take him by surprise. And when he left the house, he took with him his till, containing the takings from his business, and hid it in the yard, no doubt planning to claim that it had been lost in the fire. There was no accident, there was no danger – there was only arson and fraud." Kerr made as though to flourish with his hand, but a grim look from the judge stopped him.

"Very theatrical, Mr Kerr – thank you." Kerr sat down stiffly. Sir John now turned his attention to the wretched man Wakefield, who had listened to all the evidence in wide-eyed terror.

"You have heard what has been said about the fire, and about your insurance policy," said the judge. "You have heard the questions put by Mr Kerr, and the answers supplied to those questions. Before the jury considers its verdict, do you wish to say anything in your own defence?"

Wakefield looked about him, his eyes lighting on a pale woman who I assumed was his wife. The tears coursed unheeded down her face as she stared back at her husband.

"When I first rented from Mr Williams," began the defendant, "I asked him whether the premises were insured. An eating house has need of insurance. And he said that he had not insured the walls of the premises, and that if any accident happened he should expect me to rebuild them. And so I went to the London Assurance Company and insured the premises for four hundred and fifty pounds. Anyone would have done the same. Anyone." He came to a halt, his hands clutching the bar in front of him.

"Thank you, Mr Wakefield. The jury will now consider its verdict." Sir John turned to look at the three rows of the Middlesex jury in their high-sided box. "Gentlemen, you have one key matter to decide: was the fire accidental or deliberate? If you find it to be deliberate, then you must ask yourselves whether the defendant had the motive for committing such an act. And if you find that he did, and so is guilty of arson, then the charge of fraud against Mr Williams will also be found. Gentlemen, you may confer."

The jurymen leaned in towards each other. There was a general shuffling in the court as people adjusted their positions or took the opportunity to leave, and I spotted Wilson making his way over to me.

"How was I?" he said as I moved along the bench to make room for him.

"Clear, accurate, to the point – an excellent witness," I said. He beamed.

"What do you think for the verdict?" he asked.

"Guilty, without a doubt. As for the sentence, well, Mr Wakefield must pin his hopes on the benevolence of Sir John."

The chairman of the jury signalled to the clerk, who went up to the bench and whispered to the judge.

"You have reached a verdict?" Sir John asked. The chairman nodded.

"On the charge of arson," intoned the clerk, "how do you find?"

"Guilty."

"On the charge of fraud, how do you find?"

"Guilty."

In the dock, Wakefield stood silent.

The judge sighed; the anticipation of his next task clearly gave him no pleasure. "Mr Wakefield," he said, looking over at the dock with more compassion than most would offer a convicted arsonist. "You have been found guilty of arson and fraud. I have no alternative but to sentence you according to the law, and you are therefore sentenced to death. However," he held up his hand, "your behaviour has been penitent and I therefore order that you shall be remanded as a respite during His Majesty's pleasure." I looked at Wakefield, and at his wife: both were staring blankly at the judge. Sir John obviously saw the same incomprehension on their faces. "This means that you shall not hang immediately, but instead will go to gaol for the sentence to be carried out at a later date."

"Which means never," I explained to Wilson. "Sir John has little appetite for the noose. Mr Wakefield will spend a few months in prison, and if he stays out of trouble, Sir John will exercise the Royal prerogative of mercy and Wakefield will be pardoned. I suggest you head for the dock and explain that to the poor man – no-one else will think to do it."

CHAPTER TEN

The Turk's Head

SATURDAY 28TH MAY 1825

It is rare, in my experience, for a man's wife to encourage him to attend a public house, but I was sitting at the table examining the handle of one of Martha's cooking pots that she had complained was coming loose when she cocked her ear to the tolling of the church bell and said, "Right, you can be off now." In my shirt sleeves and plain trousers I had planned to spend the day at home, but she had other ideas, picking up my jacket and holding it out expectantly.

"Come on, Sam," she said. "The Turk's Head is waiting. Mrs Dyer said that her husband probably met whoever introduced him to the investment scheme there, and if you don't strike while the iron is hot, he might move on. It's less than a month until the trial."

It was a fair stretch of the legs to the Turk's Head and I was ready for my ale. There weren't many in when I arrived, so I tucked myself into a dark corner and waited. Not for the first time I thanked providence for giving me such an ordinary appearance – perhaps a little on the short side, to be sure, but otherwise perfectly normal in every way. When in uniform, a constable needs to be seen and his office recognised, but at other times, it is a signal blessing to draw no attention or recollection whatsoever. As noon approached, the room gradually filled with bodies and sound. A few clerks from nearby offices called in with their week's wages for some refreshment, along with various dealers and shopkeepers, and a passing traveller or two joined us. I began to understand why someone looking for investors might like the pickings in the Turk's Head.

After about an hour, the door opened and in came a young man. He acknowledged the keeper with a slight nod, allowed his eyes to adjust to the gloom, and then looked around him. Only two types of men survey a room in that fashion: constables and criminals. Indeed, we are two sides of the same coin: we share many of the same skills and much of the same experience and knowledge, but one turns it to good and the other to evil. And this was no police officer – he was too well-dressed for that. His fine cutaway coat had a velvet collar, and a snowy white cravat topped off a fancy waistcoat striped in pale and dark blue. The shine on his boots put even mine to shame, and the hat tucked under his arm must have cost several weeks' wages. His gaze took in (as had mine earlier) who had money to spare, who was being generous with buying drinks, and who was allowing that drink to get the better of him. He settled on a man of middle years, sitting alone at a table with a newspaper before him.

It was quite an education to watch the trickster at work. He was able to make his face seem open and friendly as he approached the man's table, seemingly randomly, indicating the crowdedness of the room and being offered a seat. He pointed at the newspaper and doubtless struck up a conversation on some story of the day. By judicious movements, he drew the man's attention to his own smart clothes, his cufflinks, his watch. And then he started reeling him in. It took probably half an hour, during which the trickster wrote figures on a pad, leaned forward while glancing suspiciously around the room, and generally convinced his victim that he was being vouchsafed a valuable secret. From behind my own newspaper, I saw the charlatan draw some papers and a pen from his coat pocket, and slide them across the table. The other man hesitated for a moment, and – a masterstroke this – the other made to withdraw the papers. A signature was quickly added, a handshake shared, and the deal was done. The rogue pulled out his fine watch once again, shook his head sadly and, with a reluctance so well-feigned I almost believed it myself, took his leave.

By the time I was outside, the man with the papers was halfway down Broad Street. I followed him at a careful distance from the other side of the street; like mine, his instinct for knowing when someone was watching him would be well honed. He ducked down an alleyway and I had to move sharpish to keep up. He walked smartly, obviously knowing his way around, until he reached a churchyard – St Giles, if I was not mistaken – where he stopped and waited. I walked past, turned another corner, and then peered back at him.

After a few minutes, another man joined him – and I recognised the fellow who had met the schoolmaster outside All Souls' church. The same canary waistcoat, the same air of smugness overlaid with threat. The two conferred quietly, the man from the public house handed over the signed papers, and they parted. Canary walked towards me, and I dropped quickly to the floor, as though seeing to the lace on my boot. He looked down at me, and I dared not follow him: a man such as that would have registered everything about me, and my chances of being able to shadow him undetected were now gone.

CHAPTER ELEVEN

Roast pork

FRIDAY 3RD JUNE 1825

About a week later, Wilson and I were returning to Great Marlborough Street when the chaos created by the slow progress of a wide cart along Oxford Street caused us to sidestep into one of the many little streets that criss-cross Piccadilly. Halfway along, my attention was caught by a wonderful smell of roasting meat, and I glanced across at an eating house. Written across the top of the door was the name of the proprietor: Ed. Wakefield. I pointed it out to Wilson. A slight charring on the front wall was all that suggested that the premises had, merely weeks ago, been ablaze. Obviously the arsonist's wife had managed to repair and reopen the premises while he awaited his sentence in gaol. A constable's curiosity is never off duty, and so we went in.

It was nearly noon, and the eating house was full of customers. Some were standing at the counter, eating their meals, while others were waiting for pots to be filled to take off the premises. Two cooks were sweating over the range at the back, and customers were being served by Mrs Wakefield, who – in the heat of the shop – had much more colour in her cheeks than I had seen at her husband's trial. As each order was placed, she called it over her shoulder to one of the cooks, who would then repeat it to the second cook. The effect was of one of those children's songs in the round, where everyone sings the same words but at a different time.

We backed out of the shop with some difficulty as by now hungry people were queuing into the street. Standing outside the haberdasher's next door was the proprietor, sucking on a pipe.

"Can't wait, eh?" he said to me, jerking his head towards the queue. "Might be worth it, mind you: best roast pork in Piccadilly."

Wilson licked his lips – you don't get to be his size without a decent appetite.

"Is it always this busy?" I asked.

"At noontime, aye," he nodded. "Those two cooks, they've been with the Wakefields for years, apparently – at their old premises, and then moved here with them."

"So the business has not been in trouble recently? Financial difficulties?"

The haberdasher knocked his pipe out on the side of his boot. He looked at me appraisingly. "You constables asking questions for the insurance companies these days?"

I laughed – I hoped reassuringly. "Nothing like that, no. Just making conversation." He sniffed. "I daresay you know the Wakefields well – good customers?"

It was his turn to laugh. "Good customers? I should say not. You couldn't keep a tighter grip on your purse strings than Ma Wakefield; if she orders material for a new dress, the wife and I put out the flags. She only lets him go to those lectures he's so fond of because they're free."

The queue died down momentarily, and I relented and let Wilson go in to buy a meal. Once he had polished off his plate – literally, with a piece of bread, until there was not a scrap left on it – we continued back to the office.

"So what does all of that tell us?" I asked him.

"That the haberdasher was right about the pork being good?" I gave him a look, and he tried again. "That the Wakefields' eating house is a successful business." I nodded. "And that it has been so for some time." I nodded again, and made a circular motion with my hand to indicate that I was waiting for more. Wilson shook his head.

"The haberdasher?" I prompted. Silence. "He said that Mrs Wakefield is not a good customer, that she rarely has a new dress. So let us consider the arithmetic. There is no shortage of money coming in, and not much going out. So why..."

"So why would Wakefield need the insurance money!" finished Wilson triumphantly.

"Precisely. What financial matter was so pressing that he was willing to destroy his own business and risk the scaffold?"

CHAPTER TWELVE

The respited sentence

TUESDAY 7TH JUNE 1825

Tothill Fields Bridewell had started life perhaps two centuries ago as a house of correction – to provide compulsory employment to able-bodied but indolent paupers – but by the time Edward Wakefield was sent there to await his sentence, and Wilson and I went to see him, it had become simply one of London's many overcrowded gaols. Being familiar with the routine of such places, I timed our visit to coincide with the noontime meal, when prisoners are allowed to congregate. A coin in the hand of the warder bought us access to the yard, and I soon spotted Wakefield sitting on a bench against the wall, his bowl cradled in his hand. The lad sitting next to him took in our uniforms at a glance, and melted away into the crowd. I sat down next to Wakefield, and Wilson stood to one side.

"Mr Wakefield," I began.

He peered into my face with the suspicion that I swear is issued at the door of every prison – Simple Simon himself would end up looking sideways at everyone after ten minutes in a London gaol.

"Mr Wakefield, my name is Constable Plank, and I was present at your trial."

"Why? What business was it of yours?"

"None at all, save that my junior constable here, Wilson, was to give evidence and I promised to look in on him." My companion looked past me at Wilson and sniffed. "But whatever the reason," I continued, "I was there and I heard all that was said. You received a respited sentence, is that not so?"

"That's what the judge said, yes." He was silent for a moment, obviously weighing up whether or not to trust me. He put the bowl on the floor between his feet, and suddenly his hand shot out and gripped my forearm. "Can you tell me what that means, sir? My wife has tried to see the keeper here, but no-one will talk to her – and when I ask the others," he gestured around the yard, "they just laugh and," he released my arm, "and they do this." He drew a finger across his throat. "Is that what it means? Am I to be hanged?"

I turned a little to face him. "Mr Wakefield, I am not a judge, nor a lawyer, but I have attended more trials than I care to count. And I do know that a respited sentence means that the penalty has been postponed. It is often used for pregnant women, who cannot be hanged, and so the sentence is postponed until after the birth of the child, but it is used for other reasons too. Your judge was Sir John Bayley, I recall." Wakefield nodded. "And he is among those judges who feel that the scaffold should be reserved for the most serious of violent crimes. Although he is obliged by law to pass a sentence of death when a prisoner is found guilty of arson, he will do all he can to prevent that sentence being carried out – as he has done in your case."

"So what will happen, constable? Will I stay in here for the rest of my life instead? For if that is the case, I would sooner die – then my poor wife can find another man to care for her..."

I held up my hand. "If everyone with a respited sentence was simply locked up forever, we would have to turn the whole of London into a gaol to hold them all. What happens is partly up to you, Mr Wakefield. If you are a model prisoner, if you keep yourself out of trouble and show yourself to be remorseful, in due course – a matter of months rather than years, almost certainly – your case will be brought back before Sir John. Along with other judges, he is empowered to exercise what is known as the Royal prerogative of mercy – in other words, he can pardon you. This he will do, and you will be released."

Beside me, Wakefield sat absolutely still. I thought he had not heard, or not understood, what I had said, but then a tear ran down his face. "Thank you, constable – oh, thank you."

I gave him a moment to collect himself. "As I say, Mr Wakefield, your own behaviour will have an influence on the outcome of your present situation: Sir John will wish to know that you have done all you can to make amends for your transgressions. And with that in mind, there is a small matter with which you might be able to help us." Wakefield wiped a grubby hand across his face and nodded. "Constable Wilson and I have taken an interest in your case, and we know from our enquiries that you should not have any debts: your eating house is thriving, and your expenditure is modest. And yet you were driven to extreme measures." Wakefield made no response, but he was listening. "Why, Mr Wakefield? Why did you so desperately need money?" Again, nothing. "Shall I tell you what I think, Mr Wakefield? I think you were enticed to make investments." His flinch told me I was near the mark. I looked up at Wilson and he gave the slightest of nods, indicating that he too had seen the reaction. "I think you were told that your money was safe, that the profits were guaranteed. And when no profit was forth-coming, I think you asked for your investment back, and were threatened." I paused. "Who is threatening you, Mr Wakefield? Tell us so that we can help you."

Wakefield shook his head. "I can't. He said that if I made trouble, he knew where my shop was, and he would put a torch to it. In fact," he hung his head, "that was what gave me the idea about the insurance claim."

Something suddenly occurred to me. "The man who threatened you, was he the man who originally suggested the investment to you?"

"Oh no – that was someone else entirely."

"And tell me, Mr Wakefield, did you meet this other man, the one who first told you about the investment, at an evening lecture?"

Wakefield looked at me in surprise. "I did, yes."

"At the London Mechanics' Institute?"

He nodded, and by now both he and Wilson were looking at me with amazement.

"And did this man have a limp?" His astonishment grew even greater as he nodded again. I am afraid that I enjoyed leaving him with the impression that we consta-bles see, hear and indeed know everything.

CHAPTER THIRTEEN

Plain dark material

WEDNESDAY 22ND JUNE 1825

Sometimes it felt as though I spent too many days sitting on hard benches in court rooms, watching poor wretches being dragged through the English legal system. Once, when we were first married, Martha had persuaded me – against my better judgment – to bring her with me to watch a day's business. The courts are public places, after all; anyone can turn up and see justice administered. After hours of having thieves, beggars, rogues and charlatans of every stripe paraded before her, Martha had turned to me, tears trembling on her lashes, and whispered, "Those poor, poor people." Where others might have seen wickedness and greed, my wife saw only inadequacy and misfortune. I confess that I learnt as much as she did that day.

Her words came back to me as I looked at John Dyer standing in the dock. His face showed pale against his black coat, which was shiny and worn at the elbows, and I could see tiny spots of blood where he had nicked himself shaving over the bony edges of his jaw. I glanced around for anyone who might be his wife, before remembering that as an invalid with six children, such an excursion would be impossible for her. I did however see Mr Freame the banker; he spotted me too, and inclined his head in greeting.

On the bench was Thomas Denman, Common Sergeant of London. He had a reputation as a man of liberal principles, which could work in Dyer's favour. As an experienced judge, Denman would be keen to get on with the business of the day, and indeed, as I watched, he gestured impatiently to the clerk to get on with the next case – that of the schoolmaster.

The prosecuting lawyer laid out the facts of the situation as I remembered them: that on the twenty-fifth March last a fifteen pound cheque, intended as a donation to All Souls' Charity School, had been handed to a man matching Dyer's description by a clerk at the Ironmongers' Company, and that three days later a man, again matching Dyer's description, had presented that cheque at the banking house of Messrs Freame and Company in Cheapside, and that fifteen pounds had been paid out, and that the school had received not a penny.

"Have you aught to say, Mr Dyer?" asked the lawyer, looking over his spectacles at the prisoner. Dyer shook his head.

"Pray continue, if you please, Mr Hook," said the judge. "Or is that the conclusion of the case for the prosecution?"

The lawyer looked surprised, as well he might – I could see plenty more papers in his hand, suggesting that he was only partway through his work. He gave a slight bow and turned to address the clerk, who in turn beckoned to a well-dressed man sitting on the front bench. The man took the stand and was sworn in; he gave his name as Peter Nettleton, and his occupation as tailor.

"The prisoner in the dock," said the lawyer, indicating Dyer, "have you seen him before today?"

"I have, sir, yes. In April last I made him a pair of trousers. Cossacks in plain dark material, for his work I assumed."

"Are you sure it was this man?"

"Absolutely: I remember the careful measuring I had to do, with the gentleman having a rather pronounced limp."

"And how did he pay for the trousers?"

"He gave me a five pound note."

"Is that unusual?"

"Not unusual, no – but not common."

"And what did you do with the note?"

"I wrote the gentleman's name on it – my wife takes care of the shop accounts, and it was her suggestion, to make it easier to match payments to entries in the ledger. And then, a few days later, I used it to settle our account with the butcher."

"Is this the note?" The lawyer reached under a pile of papers and produced a banknote with a flourish. He handed it to the clerk, who in turn passed it to the tailor.

Nettleton examined the banknote. "Indeed, yes: here is his name, Dyer, in my hand."

"Thank you, Mr Nettleton." The lawyer retrieved the banknote and laid it on the green baize table in front of him.

At a signal from Hook, the clerk then called another man to give evidence; this was Mr Wood, a publican. He confirmed that in early April last – he could not swear to the exact date – he had received a five pound banknote from a man.

"Did you know the man?" asked Hook.

"No, sir, I did not."

"Then how can you be sure that it was this man, the prisoner?"

"I remember that he was tall and thin, with dark hair, and a bad limp. And I wrote that on the note, in case of difficulties."

"Difficulties?"

"Well, sometimes a bank will try to claim that a note is forged when it is not, and so I have taken to writing on the note a description of whoever presents it. That is usually enough to jog their memory and make them change their mind."

Hook once again did his conjuring trick, producing a second banknote from under his pile of papers. "And is this the banknote you received from the prisoner?"

Wood examined the note. "No doubt at all. See, here I have written, 'Tall, dark, limp – early morning'. He must have come in first thing with the note."

"Thank you, Mr Wood." And Hook laid this second note alongside the first on his table. Once Wood had left the dock, Hook turned his attention to the schoolmaster. "Mr Dyer," he said, "when a police officer searched your house, he found in your bureau an envelope containing a single five pound banknote. This has been examined by the senior clerk at Freame and Company, and he has confirmed that it is one of three that he paid out against a cheque for fifteen pounds presented to him on the twenty-eighth March last. Here it is." He held up a third banknote, and then placed it alongside the other two. "Fifteen pounds, Mr Dyer – and each banknote now connected to you."

Dyer hung his head. The judge glanced over at the clerk and looked as though he was about to speak, but the clerk jumped up quickly and said, "Mr Freame, of the banking house of Freame and Company, would like to address the court and speak as to the character of the prisoner."

"Indeed," said Denman, no doubt surprised that a man such as Dyer would have anyone to defend his character. Very well, then, very well."

Mr Freame made his way to the dock, and bowed to the bench. "My name is Edward Freame, my lord, and I am the managing partner of the banking house of Freame and Company, of Cheapside. I wish to speak not of the character of this particular man, but of the character of men like him." The judge raised his eyebrows slightly at the banker, but did not interrupt. "As I understand it, Mr Dyer is a schoolmaster of twenty years' standing. During those years, he has given loyal and unstinting service to his employers, the committee of the charity school where he teaches the senior boys. In the past year, however, Mr Dyer has fallen prey to others who have convinced him to part with money." My ears pricked up at this. "Like many in his profession, Mr Dyer is an innocent in matters financial, and as his outgoings became more pressing – I am told that he has an invalid wife and six small children – he was unable to resist the promises made to him of handsome returns on small investments. It is the sadly inevitable loss of these small investments that has led him here: as his investments failed, he saw embezzlement as his only route of escape."

By now, I had my notebook open and was writing down everything the banker said; I would quiz him later to find out more. He continued.

"I am not denying that embezzlement has occurred: we have heard the fate of the three five pound banknotes, and Mr Dyer's demeanour today can leave us in no doubt as to his guilty role in this sorry matter." As one, those in the court turned to look at the pale and miserable face of the schoolmaster. "However, I prefer to reserve my ire and condemnation not for this poor wretch who, driven half-mad by financial anxiety, has trusted the promises of others, but rather for those others, those liars who have taken advantage of him and – I am certain – of many others too."

"Hear hear!" cried a man in the crowd, earning himself a stern look from both the judge and the clerk.

"As to the money, my lord, you have sitting before you now the fifteen pounds. It has been recovered, and I propose that we pass it immediately to the charity school for which it was always intended. Out of pocket we have a tailor and a publican, to whom I will pay, from our bank's resources, five pounds each. Mr Dyer has profited by a pair of ordinary trousers, and food for his family – none of which I begrudge him. I therefore submit that the sensible, the humane, the Christian thing to do is to…"

"Mr Freame," interrupted the judge, "you forget yourself. You are merely a witness in my court – it is not for you to direct how this matter is to be settled. We have here a guilty verdict, I take it?" He looked at the chairman of the jury, who, rather taken aback by the unexpected turn of events, held a hasty whispered conference with his jury brethren and then stood and nodded. "And the crime of embezzlement carries the sentence of death, does it not?" This time the clerk nodded.

It was Mr Freame who interrupted now. "And in the passing of such a barbaric and pitiless sentence, my lord, I can take no part. I will withdraw my offer of making good the loss to these two fine tradesmen," (Nettleton and Wood looked most put out at this turn in their fortune) "and I will take the matter to the newspapers. I will petition the Prime Minister, nay, His Majesty, citing your name in my petition. A man such as Mr Dyer deserves our pity and our help, and we diminish ourselves in the eyes of God if we cannot offer them." A smattering of applause ran around the court – I had to admit that Mr Freame was a fine speaker.

And he had – by pure chance, I suspected – hit home. Denman's role as one of the counsel for the late Queen in her adultery trial a few years earlier had earned him the disfavour of the King, and I fancied that he did not wish to draw more regal attention to himself. Moreover, the judge's own liberal sympathies chimed with the growing public feeling against the use of the scaffold for any but the most heinous of crimes.

"You make your point with passion, Mr Freame," said the judge after a short silence, "and I am minded to settle this matter quickly. Let it be recorded that, as Mr Dyer has a wife and six children, all of whom depend upon him, and as he is a man of previously blameless character, I recommend him to mercy. Judgment is discharged."

By the time I managed to get out of the court building, there was no sign of Mr Freame. I looked up and down the street, and just glimpsed him turning the corner into Newgate Street. I walked quickly after him, and finally caught up with him outside St Martin's le Grand.

"Ah, Constable Plank," he said warmly, tipping his hat to me. "I saw you in court. An excellent and fitting outcome I thought, was it not? I did wonder whether Sir Thomas would remember that transportation is often suggested for embezzlers – which, frankly, would have left Mrs Dyer and her little ones no better off than the scaffold – but thankfully his mind was perhaps on his dinner. And now, constable, unless there is anything else...?"

"Actually, sir, there is something I wanted to ask you." I took out my notebook. "You said that Mr Dyer had fallen into financial difficulties because he could not 'resist the promises made to him of handsome returns on small investments'." I looked up and the banker nodded. "Was that just supposition, or do you know that to be the case?"

Mr Freame cocked his head to one side, like an inquisitive sparrow. "May I ask, constable, what is your interest in this matter?"

I closed my notebook. "Mr Freame," I said, "I am not of your faith, but I have sympathy with many of your beliefs. I fear that our laws concentrate too much on the crime, and not enough on the criminal – that we too rarely take the time to discover what has driven him to do what he has done. I am fortunate enough to work for a magistrate who is likewise exercised by these considerations, and as long as my other duties are fulfilled, he encourages me to look more deeply into the ills that befall our society."

"Would that more were of his view, and then we might have more effective prevention and less need of deathly cure." The banker sighed.

"Something you said has prompted an as yet incomplete thought in my mind." I opened my notebook again. "You said that you thought that Dyer would not be the only victim of this deception."

Freame shook his head sadly. "Indeed not – I am sure of it. I will be entirely frank with you, constable. I have never met John Dyer – not before his trial, and not since. I know of him only what I could glean from the court clerk, about his family and profession. But I am a banker, and as such something of an expert in money – and the dangers thereof. In recent months, several customers have spoken to me of approaches they have received from people offering investment opportunities, in anything from steel and iron works, to canals, to gas lighting companies. They spoke of irresistible returns on their money – the repeal of the Bubble Act is to blame, you can be sure. For those who had yet to invest, I was able to warn them off, but for others it was too late. Thankfully most of my customers can stand the loss, but for others in a less fortunate position, like Mr Dyer, it would be devastating."

"But you do not know for sure that this is what happened to him?"

Freame shook his head. "A lucky guess, based on what I knew of his background, and what that told me about his character and his financial naivety, and on simple deduction: why would a man like Mr Dyer suddenly need money so desperately, and such a lot of it? A teacher with a sickly wife and large family has no time for other vices – horses, women – and so an investment gone bad seemed a distinct possibility. And you could see from his reaction, or rather lack of it, that I had hit the nail on the head."

"Why do you think that he did not explain any of this to me or to the magistrate, and so avoid a trial?"

Mr Freame drew a watch from his pocket and looked at it. "That, I am afraid, is very much your province rather than mine, constable, and now I really must make haste. To hazard a guess, I would imagine shame, or fear, but in this case, my money would be on fear. There must be something he fears more than the judge, or indeed the scaffold. Good day to you, constable," he started to move off, "and good luck."

CHAPTER FOURTEEN

The Great
Assembly Room

MONDAY 11TH JULY 1825

"Do you have your satchel and slate?" teased Martha as I readied myself. "Make sure to stay away from the naughty boys."

She had been joking in a similar vein for some days, ever since I had mentioned my intention to track down the schoolmaster Dyer at a place that I felt sure was significant. Both he and Wakefield had mentioned attending evening lectures, and so I was planning to go myself to the London Mechanics' Institute. Established only for two years it was already a roaring success, attracting audiences of more than a thousand to hear expert speakers on any subject at all except divinity and party politics (those two being considered controversial and divisive rather than educational), as well as holding classes in all sorts of disciplines, from drawing to literature to use of the globes. Indeed, it was so popular that Mr Birkbeck, the man who had founded the place, had paid for new premises which were being built on Chancery Lane, but for now I was turning my step to the Institute's current home in the Crown and Anchor tavern on the Strand. I tapped my cheek. "How about a good luck kiss for the eager pupil?" Martha obliged – she was rarely stingy with her kisses.

When I arrived just before seven o'clock, men were streaming into the Crown and Anchor. This was no drinking snug: the tavern stood four storeys high and stretched from Arundel Street to Milford Lane. Tall windows allowed the summer evening light to flood into the building. I followed the herd in through the principal entrance on Arundel Street and found myself in an elegant and spacious foyer, paved with stone and dominated by four tall columns supporting a gallery above. Dinner was in full swing in the large dining room on the ground floor, but along with the majority of the other arrivals I continued up the stone staircase with its iron railings and mahogany handrails to the second floor lobby. Above our heads were two conical skylights and an as yet unlit lantern on an epic scale. From here, we made our way into the Great Assembly Room, the venue for this evening's lecture. I had been told that it was one of the largest rooms in the metropolis, capable of holding two thousand, and I could quite believe it. A great domed ceiling rose above us, and from it on long chains hung chandeliers worthy of the finest ballroom. Indeed, this was frequently the venue for fine balls, but tonight the room was filled with chairs and benches of all varieties, no doubt pressed into service from every other room in the tavern in readiness for a very large audience.

I found myself a seat at the rear of the hall, near the door, so that I could look out for the schoolmaster. I was not certain that he would attend, but tonight's lecture had been heavily advertised, and the topic – popular political economy – was of interest to most thinking men, so I thought it likely. And sure enough, two minutes after I took my seat Dyer arrived with a man I recognised as one of his fellow schoolmasters. The pair took up places towards the front of the hall, and the lecture began. The lecturer, an excitable individual from Scotland, was a fine speaker and I enjoyed his comments and the questions that they provoked. Some of the things he said were rather fanciful, and I noted them down to relay to Martha afterwards – she would be sure to cut through the fancy language to the heart of the matter. But no matter how fascinating the lecture, I made sure to keep a careful eye on Dyer as I did not want him to leave unobserved.

When the lecture ended, we applauded generously, and several members of the audience moved to the front of the room to collar the speaker. Dyer and his companion were not among them, and I followed them downstairs and into the entrance hall before I approached them.

"Ah, Mr Dyer, isn't it?" I said, touching his arm as though we had met accidentally. He looked at me and his eyes widened in recognition. "Thank you for all of your advice regarding that petition," I continued. The other schoolteacher, who had been looking at me with curiosity, lost interest. "This is indeed a fortunate encounter. Might I trouble you for a moment of your time?" I smiled pleasantly.

Dyer turned to his friend. "This may take a little while, William – you go on without me, otherwise Ellie will wonder where you are, and I'll see you at school tomorrow." They shook hands, William tipped his hat at me, and Dyer and I were alone.

"Shall we?" I said, indicating one of the smaller rooms off the hall, where groups of men were gathered round tables, drinks before them. Dyer looked nervous. "Or would you prefer just to walk? It is a fine evening." He nodded, and we went out into the street.

We walked for some minutes in silence. "My wife called in on Mrs Dyer, about two months ago. Did she tell you?" He shook his head. "It cannot be easy for her, you know."

"You don't need to tell me about things not being easy for my wife!" he said hotly, stopping to look at me. "Do you think that I don't know what a disappointment I am, how I can barely keep the wolf from the door? Did Sarah tell your wife that she regretted accepting me, that she should have taken the parson's son instead?"

We were walking alongside a low wall which was just catching the last warm rays of the summer sun, and I indicated that we should sit. Dyer lowered himself carefully, his bad leg jutting out in front of him. He caught me looking at it. "And that thing's no help."

"The wars?"

"Nothing so glamorous – although I let the lads in my class think what they like about it. No, just born that way: the leg was trapped under me in my mother's belly, the midwife said, and it never did grow properly. To give her her due, it didn't put Sarah off. She just says she's glad of an excuse not to have to dance."

"Funny how they always know the right thing to say," I agreed. "Mrs Plank tells me that I'm the perfect height for her to kiss me without risking a sore neck." The schoolmaster smiled, but it was a thin smile, and forced. "And your wife, she didn't complain about you, you know. She's not angry or disappointed – just worried. She thinks you might have become trapped in something and now you can't escape." Dyer was looking off into the distance. His eyes narrowed momentarily, as though he had spotted something, but when I checked over my shoulder there was nothing there. "Can I say something to you, Mr Dyer? Something important?" He turned to me and nodded.

"Mr Dyer, I think you have been given a second chance. You were found guilty of a crime that, by rights, should have seen you swinging at the end of a rope." I was deliberately crude in order to shock him, and he flinched. "But you had good fortune on your side: a banker who cares more about morals than money – and you can be sure that they are rare – came to speak on your behalf, and used just the right words to arouse the sympathies of a liberal judge sufficiently for him to discharge your judgment. Someone (I am guessing Mr Freame) has spoken to the committee of your school and persuaded them to retain you. And you have a wife who has stood by you and is concerned not for the theft or the shame, but for your wellbeing." I turned to look him full in the face. "Mr Dyer, do you realise quite how fortunate you are?"

"Yes – and I also know that I do not deserve such mercy. I have brought myself low by my crimes and worse, I have brought others low." His voice was full of sorrow. I waited. "Constable, do you understand investments?" he asked after a few silent minutes.

I shrugged. "I understand the principles – someone needing money for a project asks others to provide money for it, on the promise of later profits – but I have never dared try it myself."

"Would that I had not," said Dyer with genuine regret.

"The man in the canary waistcoat?" I asked. He looked at me sharply. "Have you heard of the swell mob, Mr Dyer?"

"The swell mob? No."

"The swell mob is a group, a gang if you will, of ambitious and unscrupulous young men who prey on others. They wear flash dress – blue frock coat, blue trousers tight to the knee, coloured waistcoat with velvet collar, hat at a jaunty angle. I believe that your friend is one of the swell mob."

"Friend?" said Dyer bitterly. "He is no friend of mine, I can assure you."

"But he started out by making you think that he was, didn't he?" I asked quietly. "Mr Dyer, let me assure you: you are not the first to fall for the patter of such rogues, and you will not be the last. In fact, I strongly suspect that I know of at least one other recent victim: a young lawyer by the name of Dubois." The schoolteacher's eyes flicked towards me and then away. "He was not so robust as you: when he saw the extent of his losses, he could not face the shame. He killed himself, Mr Dyer."

"Dear God, no!" cried Dyer. "I thought he..." he stopped.

"Mr Dyer, I think the best thing is for you to tell me everything: how you became involved with the man in the canary waistcoat, what he said to you in Langham Place – and how you knew the late Mr Dubois."

CHAPTER FIFTEEN

Magpies and drovers

TUESDAY 19TH JULY 1825

Since we had worked together on the case of Henry Fauntleroy the banker the previous year, John Wontner and I had become firm friends. We started out as simply police officer and prison keeper, working together, but quickly found that we had a great deal in common – not least our desire to improve the efficiency and increase the compassion with which prisoners were treated, certainly in John's own prison, and if possible throughout London. It had become my habit to call in on him whenever I found myself near Newgate, but today I had another reason for banging on that stout door and seeking admission: we were in the middle of a period of suffocating weather.

I had known hot spells before, but this was different. For four days now, the sun had beaten down on London, relentlessly penetrating even the meanest alleyways, so that respite was almost impossible to find. Dogs slouched in corners, their tongues lolling, even the birds seemed silenced by the oppression of the heat, and on more than one occasion as I went about my business I had to stop and remove my hat as a stretcher was carried from a doorway bearing the body of yet another very old or very young person who could not survive the onslaught.

The sweat ran down my back beneath my woollen coat as I thought for the hundredth time that day that a summer version of our police uniform would be most welcome. A warder dragged open the door, nodded as he saw me – by now I was well-known to all who worked at Newgate – and beckoned me in. The relief was instant: the thick prison walls meant that the air within was kept blessedly cool.

"Aye," said the warder as he led me to Wontner's office, "the lucky ones are inside today – and it's not often you can say that. Mr Wontner's on his rounds, but he'll be back shortly."

I had been in the office only a matter of minutes, revelling in the respite from both the sun and the heat, when the door opened and in came John Wontner. Pleasure at seeing me showed on his open face, and he shook my hand heartily.

"Just passing, Sam?" he asked, glancing down at the papers on his desk. "Or are you here to oversee an admission or a release?"

"Just passing, but with a motive," I said, gratefully accepting the barley water that Wontner handed to me. I gulped it down; he gestured to me with the earthenware jug and I held out my tumbler for more. He sat down and drained his own drink, and then simply waited. As I had tried to explain to Martha, I was of the opinion that Wontner's success as a keeper, the loyalty he inspired in his warders and the respect he was given by his prisoners, was due in no small part to his calmness. Certainly he was an intelligent man, but more than his intellect, I admired his manner. In a gaol, where tempers can fray and passions ignite in an instant, the positive influence of a calm man cannot be overestimated. And indeed, as I gathered my story to tell him, I felt my own anxiety lessen: John would be sure to know what to do.

"What do you know about speculation?" I asked.

If Wontner was surprised, he did not show it. "Speculation, Sam? Surely Martha would not approve."

"Not for me, John – I take enough risks walking the streets every day. But I have been looking into some matters recently, and it seems to me that speculation might be involved." I told him about the suicide of Henry Dubois, and the schoolmaster's embezzlement, and the arson at the eating house. Wontner said nothing as I talked; he simply listened and nodded.

"Do you know anything about the specific speculation, about the investments these men made?" he asked once I had finished.

I reached into my pocket and handed over the Dubois note. Wontner read it silently. "Turn it over," I instructed. "I think it's significant that he chose that particular piece of paper. I think that he tore it up in anger or desperation, just before he killed himself, and so it was to hand when he wanted to leave those final words. And when Martha went to call on Dyer's wife…"

"Ah – Great Marlborough Street's most important yet unpaid constable!" said Wontner lightly.

I smiled foolishly. "Sarah Dyer would never have spoken so candidly to me. But she told Martha that her husband had made investments in a company." I pointed at the paper in Wontner's hand. "Perhaps a lighting company."

"And what have your enquiries revealed since then?"

"A week or so ago," I replied, "I went to the Mechanics' Institute and cornered Dyer. And it's even more fiendish than I had thought."

Wontner held up a hand. "Let me guess, Sam: Dyer himself has been recruited to entice more investors into the scheme."

I was astonished. "How did you know that?"

"It is not the first time I have heard of such a ruse. Indeed, I have had a few men like Dyer pass through here recently: all well-spoken and professional, all told that they can make good on their own losses by offering up other victims. It is a very clever fraud, Sam, very clever indeed." After a few moments, he turned to me and asked, "Do you know what this puts me in mind of?" I shook my head. "The gangs of young pickpockets that come from the rookeries." He stood and walked around his office, talking as he went. "They work in small groups on the street, don't they?" I nodded. "We know that they watch shops such as Grange's or Farrance's and observe, when the gentlemen pay, into which pocket the purse is returned; they take it by turns to follow the gentleman, passing him, so to speak, from one to another, and when the time is ripe, a fast, young boy is beckoned over and the robbery is effected."

I interrupted him. "And then the purse is given to another boy, so that if the theft has been felt or witnessed, the boy who lifted it has nothing on him."

Wontner nodded. "And after that, the purse is taken back to the rookery and handed over to the man in charge, for the takings to be shared out according to rank."

"And you think that when these lads grow up, they take these same skills and techniques…"

"And so we have our investment scheme," agreed Wontner. "More sophisticated – in that they persuade people to hand over their purses willingly – but the outcome is the same: robbery."

"If the structure is the same, the man in the canary waistcoat is one of the followers, identifying the targets and tracking them until the time is ripe for the robbery – or the investment, in this case."

Wontner nodded. "Magpies, they call them – the ones who spot the shiny targets and then chatter at them until the money is handed over."

"Magpies, eh?" I shook my head. "And what about men like Dyer, one rung down on the ladder? He simply rounds up the victims and points a – a magpie," Wontner nodded, "at them."

"Drovers – because they drive the cattle to slaughter."

I laughed. "But the magpies and the drovers aren't acting alone. There must be someone in the background, organising it all, and collecting the takings and sharing them out."

"And no doubt keeping a fine portion for himself," agreed Wontner.

There was another companionable silence. It was one of the things I most valued about my friendship with the keeper, his ability to stay quiet when there was nothing to say. I cannot abide those who babble. Wontner stood and walked around his office thoughtfully.

"Whoever planned this scheme of yours obviously has a good understanding of both the law and men's minds," he said. "He knows that if he can coerce Dyer and his like into doing the recruitment for him, he passes on the danger: he is much less likely to be uncovered if he can hide behind them. And his wager paid off, didn't it? When Dyer was uncovered, he refused to admit his guilt to the magistrate, knowing that it would lead to more questions. Instead, he chose to go to trial, knowing, or having been told, that he would not have to speak in court, and so..."

"Could not incriminate anyone else," I finished. "Just like Wakefield. He told me nothing about who was behind the scheme."

Wontner nodded. "Indeed: that man, whoever he may be, has thought this through very carefully. I daresay he promised Dyer that his wife and children would be taken care of, should the worst happen. And he also knows that a man who has lost money will do almost anything to make good that loss – and that he will be too ashamed to admit his loss or to ask for help."

"It almost makes you nostalgic for a simpler time, when robbers hid in the shadows and snatched purses."

"You yearn for your more honest criminal, you mean," said Wontner with a smile.

We were silent for a few minutes, each thinking of the enemy we now faced. Then, "Listen," said Wontner, cocking his head to one side and pointing upwards. A slow, deep rumble was making its way towards us. A couple of seconds later a loud clap of thunder cracked overhead and we both jumped and then laughed. "I never thought I would be so glad to welcome rain," said Wontner. "But you'd better get home quickly – it's going to be a real downpour."

And he was right: by the time I reached Marylebone, the rain was torrential. The gutters had filled within minutes, and filthy water was running down every surface. The sky had the yellow and purple hues of a bruise, and the clouds were split every few moments with jagged lightning. As I turned the corner into Norton Street, I saw Martha standing outside our door, her face turned upwards.

"Isn't it a relief, Sam?" she asked as I approached. And we stood there, soaked to the skin and grinning like a pair of fools.

CHAPTER SIXTEEN

The marchioness's jewels

MONDAY 8TH AUGUST 1825

If it is true that the wind drives creatures and men mad, then that first week of August would have seen Bedlam bursting at the seams. It was a hot, dry wind – coming all the way from southern France, they said – and it whipped and whistled through London for five days straight. The draymen's horses whinnied and stamped their discomfort as the foetid gusts swirled around them, while the livestock being driven through the streets bleated and bellowed their unease and took every opportunity to break away from their herders. And the dust! Even Martha threw up her hands in despair after three days of passing a damp cloth over every surface only to have to start again the moment she had finished.

133

It clawed at your throat and gritted in your teeth and scratched at your eyes, and no amount of water could dislodge it. All night long the chimneys howled and every shutter and door that was not firmly barred crashed and banged fit to wake the Devil. It was too hot to have the windows closed, and too windy to have them open – and as a result, by the Monday morning when the gales had finally blown their worst and left us in peace, I was not the only one at Great Marlborough Street who was short on sleep and therefore of temper.

"He wants to see you," said Thomas Neale, jerking his head in the direction of the stairs leading to Mr Conant's rooms. "A delicate case, apparently, needing your light touch." He snorted. "A criminal's a criminal, far as I'm concerned."

Thing certainly were out of sorts if our mild office-keeper's generous store of sympathy was empty.

"Come now, Tom, that's not like you," I chided. "Don't let the young lads hear you saying that, or they'll stop thinking for themselves and we'll be back to the bad old days of thief-takers."

"Aye, there's something in that," he said grudgingly. "I'm just glad that wind's died down – I'm dog-tired. I'm hoping for a busy day, so that I don't fall asleep right here at my counter – and it's not often I wish for that."

Wealth and position apparently offered little protection from the wind, for John Conant looked as smudge-eyed and slope-shouldered as the rest of us. He was at his table, as usual, reading through a stack of papers, as usual, and indicated that I should take a seat until he had finished. I have rarely met a man more hardworking than this magistrate; many holding that office rely on their clerks to feed them the essential facts of the day as they turn up in court, but Conant, he was different. You owe it to the man or woman before you, he had once explained to me, to understand as much as you can about their situation before you pass judgment on them. If you cannot walk in their shoes, you can at least read their stories.

"What a night, eh, Sam?" he said as he turned over the last sheet in the pile and removed his spectacles. "I had a horse kick a hole in the wall of his stable, he was so unsettled. Not really a day for dealing with delicate matters, perhaps, but deal with them we must." He turned to another set of papers. "Are you familiar with Lord Walsham?"

"Not personally," I said – viscounts were generally not part of my circle.

"Well, he's rarely in London these days. His estates in," he replaced his spectacles and looked down at a sheet of paper, "Northumberland occupy most of his time. As I recall, he was never much for dining and dancing – prefers foxhounds and fishing. Lady Walsham, on the other hand, well, I doubt she could locate Northumberland on a map. She spends her time at Walsham Place near St James's Park, along with their son, the Honourable George Knapton. Young George is just twenty and, according to Lily, the pinkest of the pinks, spending a fortune following every twist and turn of fashion, and, as a consequence, seems to be an utter nincompoop."

Mr Conant's daughter Lily was a valuable source of information to us when it came to matters of fashion and society. A dark-haired beauty with a ready laugh, she had inherited her father's keen intellect and his eye for detail, which meant that he enjoyed her company tremendously, and despaired of ever finding a suitor to meet her (and, to be honest, his own) exacting standards.

Conant stood and walked over to the fireplace. "Apparently the allowance Knapton receives from his father is no longer sufficient. I was summoned to see Lady Walsham last week, and then this morning she sent a note." He returned to the table and handed me a letter.

"Dear Mr Conant," I read, "Concerning the matter of which we spoke last week. Further items have gone missing, including a necklace of which I am particularly fond. You may therefore proceed as you wish, on the strict proviso that my husband is not to be informed."

"It seems that the Honourable George has been pilfering things from his mother's jewellery box. And before you ask," said Conant, seeing my expression, "thorough enquiries have been made and it is not one of the servants. In fact," and I swear Conant was trying not to smile, "I saw him do it with my own eyes. Quite ridiculous, I know, but Lady Walsham insisted that I secrete myself in her dressing room behind a curtain, and sure enough, within an hour, her son had come in and helped himself to a bracelet."

"Hardly a master criminal, then, sir," I said. "But surely all Lady Walsham needs to do is have him followed to whatever pawnbroker he is using, or whichever bird of paradise he is trying to seduce, and reclaim the items. I take it that she is not seeking to prosecute?"

"Of course not. I imagine she would rather go to a ball at the palace completely unadorned than expose her family to such scandal. No, it seems that she has had her son followed, on several occasions, and he is handing over the jewellery not to a pawnbroker or to a ladybird, but to men."

"Men? Nothing more specific than that?"

"Well-dressed men. Young men. Different, well-dressed, young men on each occasion." He looked at me, and I raised an eyebrow. "Lady Walsham fears they may be gentlemen of the back door, and has asked me to find out what is going on, to release her son from whatever entanglement has snared him, and not to alert her husband, who is liable to gallop back from the country brandishing a horsewhip." He sighed and shook his head. "But

Lily's comments suggest that Knapton's preferences are entirely normal; apparently no woman under forty is safe from his somewhat inexpert attentions. The role of an aspiring Don Juan would be quite a charade to maintain – and requiring rather more mental agility than Knapton seems to possess."

"So gambling, perhaps?"

"Aye, perhaps," said Conant, "but then why not simply gamble at his club? He's a member of White's, and their tables are legendary."

"White's? Isn't that where Lord Alvanley made that ridiculous wager?"

"Three thousand pounds on which of two raindrops would reach the bottom of the window first." Conant rolled his eyes. "So with a betting book like that, why would Knapton need to go anywhere else?"

"Blackmail, then," I suggested.

"That was my conclusion too," agreed Conant. "But as we know, blackmailers are ever greedy, and the demands will simply grow. Fop though he may be, Knapton is still worthy of our concern. And if someone is threatening him, you can be sure they are targeting others too. So, constable, can I leave it to you to conduct your usual discreet enquiries?"

CHAPTER SEVENTEEN

Riding on a tiger

WEDNESDAY 24TH AUGUST 1825

If I had known that the outing would necessitate my being shoved out of bed at such an early hour, and pestered to within an inch of my life about which shirt I was wearing and had I shaved closely and did I really think the shine on my boots was good enough, I might have thought twice about proposing it.

The Bartholomew Fair had been taking place in Smithfield for hundreds of years. Once a cloth fair, it had now become more of an entertainment – and along with the puppet shows, fire-eaters and dancing bears came all manner of light-fingered individuals intent on relieving the pleasure-seekers of their money and valuables. In particular, Bartholomew Fair was a happy hunting ground for the gangs of pickpockets operating out of nearby Bunhill Row and Grub Street. Mr Conant and his

fellow magistrates were of the opinion that having constables in attendance, in uniform and wandering through
the crowds, would serve as a warning – or at least mean
that we were on hand to respond promptly to any call of
distress.

When she heard that I was to attend the fair Martha
had asked to accompany me and I had readily agreed, little
anticipating the frenzy of preparation that such an outing
would entail. On closer questioning, it turned out that,
the year before her mother died, Martha's father had
promised to take them to Bartholomew Fair. All the children had been dressed in their finest, including a seven-
year old Martha, having not slept a wink the night before
– and the outing had come to nought. Her father, true to
form, had drunk the takings from the inn of which he was
keeper, leaving not a penny to spare for food, let alone
fairs. The disappointment had cut deep. As I spat on my
boot and polished it for the third time, I watched Martha
pin and re-pin her bonnet and then caught her round the
waist as she bustled past me.

"There now, girl – you look a picture," I said, leaning
in for a kiss. She swatted me away, but I could tell from
the flush in her cheeks that she was pleased.

"Boots," she commanded. I showed her. "They'll do.
Now do stop wasting time, Sam, or we'll be late – I don't
want to miss the arrival of the Lord Mayor."

As we walked eastwards, the streets became gradually more crowded. Whereas once upon a time the fair had been confined to the one street, it had grown and spread and now covered four whole parishes around St Bartholomew's. The heavy August sun was finding its way between the close-set buildings, and I could feel the sweat trickling down my back. The uniform of a constable may be smart, but it is certainly not light. At my side, Martha looked much fresher in her spotted muslin frock, and I felt proud to have such a woman on my arm. I had persuaded her against bringing a basket, explaining that it would be easy prey for pickpockets, and instead her reticule swung between us. I had also comforted myself that it takes many fewer purchases to fill a reticule than a basket, but despite that my chances of keeping Martha away from the stalls offering everything from toys to mousetraps, from caged birds to tumbling puppies, were slim.

As the crowds grew thicker, Martha pressed closer to me. We didn't spot the Lord Mayor himself, but Martha was delighted to see his coach and six as he was driven away, having, as I told her, already stopped at Newgate for a traditional cup of sack with the keeper, my old friend John Wontner. By then, after our long walk, we were both feeling peckish.

"Had you let me bring my basket, Sam, I could have brought some cold meat and bread from home, but as it is, you will have to put your hand in your pocket," said my wife, steering me towards a particularly busy stall. "That roast pork smells just delicious."

And for the next couple of hours I had the pleasure of seeing my wife become a young girl again. She laughed as conjurors pulled yards of scarves out of their mouths, and looked on in half-terror as tightrope walkers passed over our heads and contortionists bent and twisted as though they had no bones. When a caged tiger growled at her she hid behind me, and then shed a quiet tear for him, alone as he was and far from home. The noise was deafening: fiddles, drums and rattles played ceaselessly, while stallholders yelled and whistled to entice us to buy their beer and tobacco, their pies and sweetmeats. A loud trumpeting caught our attention, and following it we came across an elephant – an elephant! – pulling corks out of bottles with his trunk. Sitting on a throne in a scarlet tent nearby was a gypsy woman, a glittering scarf about her head, beckoning in passersby to cast their horoscopes.

"Who would want to know their future?" said Martha, shaking her head at the woman. "If it's bad, you'll waste your life worrying, and if it's good, it will be a lovely surprise."

Men in sombre clothing and tall hats, claiming the greatest medical expertise, hawked all manner of miraculous cures. And we passed several tents coyly labelled 'Soiled doves', into which men would disappear after checking guiltily over their shoulders. Martha caught me looking at one such tent, and sniffed. "Soiled indeed – heaven only knows what filth they will pick up in there. Perhaps we should direct them to Dr Foster's Supreme Salve for All Ills."

As the sun continued its relentless climb overhead, we turned a corner and found a carousel set up on a patch of grass. A tall striped pole had been driven into the ground, and suspended from this by chains was a large wooden ring. Mounted on the wooden ring was an entire menagerie of brightly-painted animals; as it spun before my eyes, I saw a fine stallion, a high-stepping zebra, a lion with a regal mane, and a giraffe with an impossibly long neck. Inside the wooden ring, pushing against spurs jutting out from the striped pole and thereby turning it for all they were worth, were ten sweating lads, working in pairs. Martha looked at me. "Shall we, Sam?"

I shook my head. "Not in uniform, my dear – not really suitable. But you have a ride, and I will wave to you as you fly past."

When the ride slowed, I paid the money to one of the lads and helped Martha onto a tiger showing a ferocious set of teeth, tucking her skirt in around her legs. The speed picked up, and she had to sacrifice one hand from the beast's reins in order to hold onto her bonnet, leaving her no hands free to wave at me. But she was squealing with laughter, and when I finally helped her from her mount, she staggered against me.

"Those poor lads," she gasped as we walked away. "Dripping with sweat, they were, and trying to keep an eye on the money too. I wonder how they remember who has paid?" She flapped her hand in front of her face. "Let's find a drink, Sam – I'm parched."

But I had stopped dead. Of course! That was the nub of the matter. The only ones keeping track of who had paid what were the ones running the machine – the riders themselves were too busy enjoying the thrill to notice whether their neighbour was getting a longer ride than they were.

CHAPTER EIGHTEEN

The missing schoolmaster

FRIDAY 26TH AUGUST 1825

Two days after our excursion to the fair, I arrived home, looking forward to the mutton stew that Martha had promised. My breakfast bacon seemed a distant memory, and my stomach was rumbling. But as I opened the door an apron-less Martha rushed up to me and barred my way. Over her shoulder, I could see a pale woman with curling fair hair and nervous hands sitting at our table and dabbing her eyes with a handkerchief.

"Sarah Dyer," said Martha in an undertone. "Her husband's gone missing." Glancing towards the visitor, Martha called out with forced gaiety, "Sam's here now, Sarah – he'll be in to talk to you in a moment. I just need to..."

and she pushed me back out of the door and pulled it to behind her. "Oh Sam, thank goodness you're here. She's in a terrible state, not making much sense. I told her you would know what to do, but she keeps saying that she mustn't report it. So I've promised her," and here she looked up at me with pleading eyes, "that you will be just my husband, and not a constable."

"But she knows that I am a constable?"

"Oh yes, I told her that when we first met. And she'll be grateful for your knowledge, I'm sure. But I promised her that you wouldn't tell anyone else what she tells you – no-one at the police office, I mean." Martha started tugging at my uniform coat. "So let's get rid of this, shall we, and then you can come in."

Looking at the two women sitting side by side, I wondered what had attracted Dyer to her, for Sarah Dyer still looked girlish and unformed, despite her six children. I have always favoured women with shape and substance, with curves to excite me and arms to enclose me. But some men liked to feel protective, and maybe Dyer, with his own physical limitations, had chosen a wife who needed him.

"Mrs Dyer," I started in my gentlest voice, "Martha tells me that you are concerned about your husband."

Our visitor nodded and sniffed, but said nothing. Martha patted Sarah's hands where they lay clasped in her lap. "Come now, Sarah – Sam is a good man. You have nothing to fear from him."

Sarah gave a small nod and bit her lip. I needed to find a way to reassure her.

"I understand that you have quite a brood of little ones," I said conversationally. "Six, is it not?"

"Yes, six," she said quietly.

"And who is with them now?" I asked.

"My sister has come up from Portsmouth – she arrived this noon."

"So your husband has been missing for a few days already, if you have had time to get word to your sister?"

Sarah nodded, a tear working its way down her cheek.

"When did you last see John, Sarah?" I asked.

"Tuesday morning, as he left for school – same as always. He looked in to say goodbye as I was feeding the baby, and then..." She started to cry quietly.

"Did he seem worried or distracted, or did he say anything in particular that seemed odd to you? Think carefully, Sarah: it may be important."

"You were feeding the baby – then what?" prompted Martha.

Sarah closed her eyes, the better to picture the scene. "I was cradling Jack, and he had just finished and was falling asleep. John looked around the door and said," she opened her eyes and flushed a little, "well, he said that he loved me and that he would be late home because he was going to one of his lectures with another schoolmaster."

"At the Mechanics' Institute?" I asked.

"I should think so," replied Sarah, nodding eagerly. "Why? Do you think they might know something?"

"It is certainly worth asking," I said. "I will go there tomorrow myself – as a concerned friend, rather than as a constable," I added quickly as I saw the fear on her face.

"It's very unlike John," she said, turning to Martha to emphasise her point. "He would not go off without telling me – he knows that I would be worried."

"Does he have any family in London, or good friends with whom he might go and stay?" I asked.

She shook her head. "Only the other schoolmasters. Since we arrived in London, what with the children and his work, he barely has time for other people – just his lectures, and an occasional drink at the Turk's Head. And before you ask, no, he is not a drunkard." She drew herself up. "John is a good and fine man, and I am sure that he is being kept from home against his will."

I was pleased to see her regain some control and determination. Martha obviously felt the same way, and she rose to her feet. "Well, now, Sarah – Sam will do what he can, and in the meantime, I will walk you home and, yes, let me see…"

As Martha moved around the kitchen, filling her basket with whatever we could spare for the Dyer children, Sarah Dyer looked me straight in the eye.

"It's to do with this investment business, isn't it?" she asked. I stayed silent. "Everything was fine before he became mixed up in that; we were struggling but managing, and John was, well, John. Since he took up with whoever he has taken up with, he has been different – snappish, and nervous. Please, Mr Plank, oh please: find my John and bring him home to us, and stop them doing this to anyone else."

CHAPTER NINETEEN

All ears

SATURDAY 27TH AUGUST 1825

Martha and I often went for a walk on Saturday afternoons. Like me, my wife marvelled at the way our metropolis grew around us. I liked grand buildings and she was fond of parks and flowers, so between us we generally managed to find a route that pleased us both. The day after Sarah Dyer's visit, however, there was no talk of leisurely strolls: the minute she had cleared our breakfast dishes, Martha pinned on her hat and turned to me, clapping her hands.

"Come on, now, Sam – you promised Sarah that you would call at the Mechanics' Institute to ask about her husband. And I would like to see this great assembly room that you talked about."

151

Martha's curiosity is one of the things that makes her an excellent wife for a constable – well, for any man, as a woman with a lively mind is a thousand times more interesting than her dull-witted sisters. No man can stagnate alongside a wife who is constantly asking why, and when, and who. The Covent Garden nuns were still plying their trade as we made our way through the close tangle of streets and alleyways; I knew Martha would exhibit no false prudery around them, but I felt her grip tighten a little on my arm as a rough-looking pimp took hold of one of his girls and pulled her into a dark doorway.

"Children, Sam, that's all some of them are – just children," she said sadly.

It was a relief to burst out onto the sunlit breadth of the Strand. We paused for a moment to look at the display of prints and knick-knacks in the windows of Ackermann's, and then stopped again outside Exeter Change, sheltering from the sun under its generous arcade. I asked Martha if she wanted to visit the menagerie upstairs, but just then one of the big cats roared and she shook her head.

We paused again when we reached Somerset House to admire its grand pillared façade. Martha rested on a low wall and ate an elderflower ice that I had bought from a seller on the corner, licking the sweetness from her fingers. When she had rinsed her hands in a horse trough, we walked on a few minutes more and reached the Mechanics' Institute.

As it had been before, the dining room was crowded with people. But I spied a little table by a window and steered Martha to it. I ordered a pot of tea and two pastries, and enjoyed the surprise on my wife's face.

"Samuel Plank," she said as she poured my tea, "you must have money to burn coming to places like this. At least I know you're not up to your neck in speculation, if you can afford ices and pastries on the same day." But I could tell that she was pleased to be drinking a cup that she had not had to brew.

Duly refreshed, we walked up the grand staircase – Martha exclaimed at the railings, and nearly cricked her neck gazing up at the lantern – and found our way to the office. Seated at a desk at the back was a rotund gentleman in shirt-sleeves, with spectacles perched precariously on the very end of his nose, poring over some paperwork. I knocked on the counter top, and he stood quickly and then shrugged on his coat when he caught sight of Martha. She inclined her head in approval – very keen on manners is my Martha.

The man came to the counter and drew a large ledger towards him. "I take it you are here to subscribe to a class, sir," he said, looking around for a pen. "I had one here not a moment since…". He returned to his desk, retrieved a pen, came back to the counter and looked up at me expectantly.

"No, not exactly," I explained. "If you please, I am seeking some information."

"Information, to be sure. Information on classes – now, where is that timetable..."

And back to his desk he went again, opening and closing drawers until "A-ha!" he exclaimed and extracted a sheet of paper covered in close type. He brought it to the counter and handed it to me. "All of our current classes, sir."

I tried again. "Not information about classes, no – information about lectures."

"Lectures – of course! How foolish of me, " said our friend, and it was back to the desk, back to the drawers, and back to us with another sheet of paper. I tried not to catch Martha's eye, as I could feel her suppressed laughter beside me.

"Please, sir, if you will let me explain," I said.

He nodded enthusiastically. "All ears, sir, I'm all ears. You have already our schedule of classes and our list of lectures, but if there is something more you require, you have only to ask. I seek to serve. All ears, sir, I'm all ears."

"I am a constable..."

"An admirable profession sir, to be sure – admirable."

"...acting on the instructions of the magistrate John Conant Esquire of Great Marlborough Street..."

"A fine part of town, Piccadilly. One of the finest –
except for this part of town."

"...and I am trying to find a gentleman, a schoolmaster..."

"Ah, how I would have enjoyed being a schoolmaster.
But alas, I am not fond of children – books and learning,
yes, but children, sadly, no. And so you see, this is the
perfect place for me." He opened his arms wide to take in
the whole Institute. "Books and learning in abundance,
but no children. Perfect, perfect."

"...who is a regular visitor to this Institute." I paused,
but the man was silent – and by now Martha was pressing
her handkerchief to her mouth. "This gentleman has now
gone missing..."

The smile fell from the man's face. "Missing? Gone
from home? How terrible, terrible! And is he a family
man, with little ones waiting sad-eyed for their papa?"
Martha and I nodded in unison. "How terrible. I am not
fond of children myself, but I am perfectly content for
other people to have them. And those who trouble to
have them should not then disappear. How may I be of
assistance in this grave matter, sir? All ears, I'm all ears."

"This man's wife has told us that the last time she saw
him was on the morning of Tuesday last, as he left for
work."

"The lady on the doorstep, surrounded by her little chicks, waving farewell to the gallant schoolmaster – a touching picture, sir, to be sure."

"And he said that he would be home rather later than usual because he was coming here, to a lecture."

"Impossible!" said the man hotly, slapping his hand on the counter. "Forgive me, madam, for suggesting that this schoolmaster was telling an untruth, but he was – or perhaps he was mistaken in the day. Yes, that must have been it: I cannot believe that a schoolmaster would tell a deliberate lie. Such an honourable profession. One I might have been drawn to myself. But not fond of children, as I say."

"Mr…" I said firmly.

"Baines, sir, Nathaniel Baines at your service."

"Mr Baines, why are you so certain that our schoolmaster was wrong?"

Baines laid his hand on the two pieces of paper that he had put on the counter, and swivelled them so that I could read them. He pointed at a specific entry on each of them. "Tuesday the twenty-third August. Five classes, but no lectures. Not a one."

"Perhaps Mr Dyer meant a class rather than a lecture, or maybe his wife misremembered what he said," suggested Martha to me.

"Both excellent suggestions, madam – excellent," said Baines approvingly. "And the work of a moment to check." He ducked down behind the counter and hauled another large ledger up onto the surface. "Current subscriptions," he said, "while that one," he pointed at the one already on the counter, "is future subscriptions. If you would be so kind, sir, could you call out the list of classes advertised for that day, and I will check the subscriptions for each, looking for your schoolmaster. His name, if you please?"

One by one we went through the classes that had been held that Tuesday evening – arithmetic, mechanics, English composition, book-keeping and history of the ancients – but there was no John Dyer in any of them. Baines shut his ledger with regret. "Alas, it seems that there was no reason for your schoolmaster to be here that evening. A sad business: we at the Institute are not in the business of losing gentlemen who come to us to better themselves." He shook his head. "Those poor children. Not fond of them myself, but still."

I thanked Mr Baines for his assistance, and Martha and I managed to escape from the Institute and turn the corner before dissolving into laughter, clutching at each other and hooting. As soon as one of us managed to gain control, the other would say, "All ears!" and we would both start again. Eventually, Martha took out her handkerchief and was wiping her eyes when she suddenly stopped.

"Look, Sam," she said urgently. I followed her gaze. Outside the Institute was a notice-board, with the class and lecture timetables that we had seen upstairs fixed to it. And alongside them was a large advertisement. "Investment Opportunity for Discerning Gentlemen!" said the headline. Underneath it continued: "A Limited Opportunity to Profit from the Industry of the Future! Large Rewards for Those Who Dare! Come to a meeting at the Crown and Anchor tavern in the Strand – Friday the second of September at eight o'clock. Arrive early: space is limited."

CHAPTER TWENTY

The godsend

FRIDAY 2^(ND) SEPTEMBER 1825

A week later I was back at the Crown and Anchor. I had considered taking Martha with me, but she said that a woman might be conspicuous at such a gathering and she was right. As Wilson and I entered the room opposite the dining room – a notice tacked on the door-frame indicated where the meeting was to be – there was not a single woman in the place.

Wilson had done me proud. I had explained only the bare bones of what we were doing, and had instructed him to dress carefully: nothing that would give him away as a constable, and something that would suggest that he had more money than sense. Heavens only knows from whom he had borrowed the silk top hat and generous cravat, but they certainly did that. My own outfit was more restrained; I was hoping to convey the impression of a man of quiet and cautious means. We greeted each other as old friends well met, and procured seats near the front with a good view of the proceedings, but not so prominent as to draw excessive attention.

There was no doubting the popularity of the meeting; by the time of the advertised start, men were still crowding in at the back, and with all seats taken they had to line the walls. At the front was a long table covered with a cloth, and behind it were ranged three seats, as yet unoccupied. At ten past the hour, three men walked to the desk; two sat, while the one in the middle remained standing. He held up his hands for quiet, and the room settled.

"Gentlemen, welcome. Thank you for your attendance this evening. Your confidence in the opportunity we are offering is both flattering and, if you will permit, well-placed." He bowed slightly. "My name is Francis Welby, and my purpose here tonight is to introduce to you our two speakers. First we will hear from Mr John Grigson," he indicated the man to his right, "who will tell you of his experience of investing in our scheme. And then it will be the turn of Mr Bartholomew Knight," indicating to his left, "who will explain how you too can take advantage of this outstanding opportunity. Mr Grigson, if you please."

John Grigson rose to his feet as Welby sat. Grigson was what you might call a solid merchant: tall and heavy-set, with well-tended whiskers and conservative dress. His deep, slow voice and calm manner put me in mind of a doctor or a pastor, and I felt sure that he had been chosen to give just this impression of reliability and trustworthiness. He spun us a pretty tale of years of hard and steady work – "up with the lark and to bed with the owl, gentlemen, and barely a moment to breathe" – with very little to show for it.

"We did not starve, gentlemen, not for a moment – my wife had a weekday hat and one for Sundays, and all the children were shod – but there was nothing left over. And nothing in the kitty for when I was ill, or to keep us in our old age." He shook his head sadly, and many in the audience murmured in sympathy, no doubt reflecting that they found themselves in the very same position. "And then, gentlemen, I heard of an opportunity to invest in an industry of the future – to add my little amount of money to a great endeavour, and to reap the benefits along with others. A scheme, they called it – a godsend, I call it!" He smiled broadly, and was rewarded with a few chuckles from the crowd. "The industry, gentlemen, is gas lighting." He paused for the revelation to sink in.

"Gas lighting, gentlemen," he continued. "We live in the greatest city on Earth. Every day people come to London in search of employment and prosperity, and every day the metropolis grows around us. Grand buildings," he threw his arm over his head to indicate the very one in which we were gathered, "wide streets, new houses and hospitals and churches and schools. And they all cry out for one thing: light. Imagine sitting in your own parlour at night and being able to read your newspaper as clearly as when you sit outside at noon. Imagine offices and shops able to open and trade during the hours of darkness. Imagine factories able to work through the night. The demand is there. Gas lighting, gentlemen, is what makes this possible – and your investment is what makes gas lighting possible. And as a reward for your perspicacity and confidence, these fine gentlemen here will take your modest investments and turn them into profit, just as they did for me." He reached down the table and heartily shook the hands of Mr Welby and Mr Knight, and the audience applauded loudly.

Wilson leaned towards me. "Gas lighting?" he asked. "Like on Westminster Bridge?" I nodded as Mr Knight stood. He was a much more flamboyant fellow, with abundant curly blonde hair, and he took a moment to pass his hands over this coiffure and then adjust his cuffs and the points of his emerald green waistcoat before he started to speak.

"I am extremely grateful to Mr Grigson for his generous endorsement," he bowed down the table, "but I must correct him on one important detail. Gas lighting is not an industry of the future." He paused to allow us time to look at each other in confusion. "No, gentlemen – it is the industry of today. Gas lighting is already commonplace in Paris, and up in Lancashire the Preston Gaslight Company has been in operation for nearly a decade. It seems ridiculous, does it not, that our capital city is being outstripped by the provinces." There were nervous laughs in the room. "Of course there are companies operating here in London. Between them, the City Gas Works and the Chartered Gas Company, for instance, are supplying eighty-four thousand gas lights, which is no small number – but still it is only a fraction of the potential. These companies are flourishing at the moment, for gas lighting costs only a quarter the price of oil lamps or candles, and the quality of luminescence is much higher. But what will make them fail, gentlemen – and you can be sure that they will fail – is the purity of their product." Here Knight leaned forward and placed his knuckles on the table, in the manner of a man sharing confidential information with a trusted few.

"We at the West London Lighting Company have invented a brand new way of purifying coal gas. I cannot go into details, of course," he looked over his shoulder, as though alert to spies, "but it is revolutionary, involving," he leaned further forward, and much of the audience likewise leaned towards him, "ammoniacal gas and iron retorts. With this method, our gas lighting will be the cleanest ever." I could imagine Henry Dubois attending just such a meeting; the very purity of the product would have appealed to his fastidious nature. "But we cannot do this without building a new gas works, and for this we need you. By buying shares in this gas works, gentlemen – and building work is to begin imminently – you will become eligible for a corresponding portion of the profits. The more shares you buy, the more profit you will make. But time is limited: once we start the building work, the share register will be closed, and future profits will be divided only among those already subscribed. It would be manifestly unfair to allow others to join later, once the profits are there for all to see, and claim the same reward as those gentlemen – as you, gentlemen – who have shown the foresight to invest at the launch of our venture."

Knight sat down to another round of generous applause. Welby stood again.

"I would like to thank both Mr Grigson and Mr Knight for sparing us their valuable time this evening," he said. "As you are no doubt convinced, gentlemen, we are offering you the opportunity to contribute to a most important development, but I must stress once again that we cannot offer this opportunity for long. Others have already invested," he indicated Grigson, who smiled and nodded, "and we need only a few more contributions to reach our target, at which point we will be closing the share register. Now, I am sure you are all keen to know how to make your investments, and if you look to the back of the room," we all obligingly turned around, "you will see that there are two tables. At each table is one of my colleagues, and he will take your name and explain all the practical details." Barely were the words out of his mouth than several men in the audience stood and started to push their way to the back of the room. "And so, gentlemen," continued Welby above the increasing noise, "may I thank you once again for your attendance this evening, and I look forward to sharing with many of you the happy – and profitable – future of the West London Lighting Company."

I nudged Wilson. "Quick – you need to get to one of those tables before they pretend that they have enough investors. Remember the name and address we agreed."

Wilson clapped his hat on his head and set off. I went against the flow of the crowd and walked to the front of the room, feigning interest in the wall decorations. The three speakers were huddled together, no doubt dissecting the evening's events, when a side door opened and in came a fourth man and approached them. I turned away quickly before he saw me – no point showing my face to anyone who doesn't need to see it – but I certainly saw him. It was the swell who had met, and threatened, Dyer outside All Souls' in Langham Place: it was the man in the canary waistcoat.

I made my way to the back of the room and indicated to Wilson that I would wait for him outside. Once there, I paused to enjoy the fresh night air – the meeting room had grown rather stuffy. After about ten minutes, Wilson joined me.

"Well?" I asked. "What happened?"

"Quite simple, really," replied Wilson, shrugging. "I had to add my name and address to a list, and the man congratulated me on making a wise decision, and said that someone would call tomorrow at six o'clock to collect my subscription and give me my share certificate."

"Samuel Williams, and my address?" Wilson nodded. "Good. So you will wait at my house tomorrow evening, meet whoever is sent, and then you and I will follow him to whoever is in charge."

"So you don't think it's Mr Welby?" asked Wilson.

I shook my head. "No, I think we are dealing with the drones. We need to find the queen – or more likely, king – bee. And tonight we made a very good start."

Wilson looked pleased, and tipped his fancy top hat to a rakish angle. I pointed at it.

"Where's that from?" I asked.

"I borrowed it from Jem Butler," he said.

"The jarvey?"

He nodded. "Apparently a gent flashed the hash in his cab a few nights ago, and Jem said that he is holding the hat to ransom until the fool comes back and pays him for all the extra work he had cleaning out the cab. But Jem didn't want to be accused of stealing, so he brought the hat to us in the police office for safekeeping, and I just borrowed it for this evening."

I shook my head. "And the cravat?"

"Ah well," said Wilson with a broad smile. "That was my sister Sal's idea. It's her best Sunday petticoat, all cleverly folded so that the lace bits are inside my waistcoat."

"Well, well, Constable Wilson," I said as we headed for home. "That's quite some ammunition you've given me there. Step out of line, and I might just have to tell everyone at the police office that you go out of an evening dressed in women's undergarments."

CHAPTER TWENTY-ONE

Bow windows and barred ones

MONDAY 5TH SEPTEMBER 1825

"Constable Wilson is certainly doing well under your tutelage," said Mr Conant, shaking his head as I told him about our outing to the investment meeting the previous evening. "But keep an eye on him, Sam. Young men are apt to underestimate danger."

"I will not leave him alone with his caller," I reassured the magistrate. "I will overhear everything they say, and once the man has left, Wilson and I will follow him together."

"What about the money? The investment?" he asked, walking over to his table and glancing at some papers.

"Our visitor will find that, sadly, Mr Williams has had second thoughts. He will be disappointed, naturally, but I doubt he will cut up rough – Wilson is an imposing fellow."

Conant nodded absently as he read something on his table. "And what about this schoolmaster – any sign of him?"

I shook my head. "Nothing, sir. I was wondering whether the offer of a reward might help."

Conant looked at me sharply. "A reward? For a schoolmaster?"

"For a schoolmaster who has been threatened by the same man I saw at our gathering yesterday," I pointed out.

"Perhaps," conceded Conant. "How much were you thinking?"

"Two guineas is customary."

"Dead or alive?" I nodded. "Very well," said Conant, waving his hand. "Have the notices printed, and send the lads with them to all police offices." He looked up at me. "Is there anything else?" I shook my head. "In that case, I look forward to hearing about your visitor this evening – and look after that young constable of yours."

Martha had rolled her eyes when I told her of our plan, but she didn't object; her indignation at the distress of Dyer's wife and children made her nearly as determined as I was that those responsible should be found. Wilson arrived at five o'clock, ducking his head as he came into the kitchen and looking as awkward as he always did in small rooms. Martha pushed him down onto a chair, put a plate of meat and potatoes in front of him, and indicated that he should cut himself some bread. He was once again wearing the petticoat-cravat, and I could see Martha eying it with amusement. My own appetite was rather poor – nerves, I suppose – but I drank some beef broth. After clearing and rinsing the plates, Martha put on her hat.

She put her hand on my arm. "Now, you take care of him, won't you?" she said to me in a low voice, nodding towards Wilson. "He's not nearly as wily as you are." She looked over at him, using a piece of bread to soak up some gravy and then leaning right over the plate to avoid dripping it on his cravat. "And you, William," she said in the tone of mothers everywhere, "Do as Sam tells you and take care of yourself. These men might dress fancy, but they're common rogues through and through – and rough with it." She gave a curt nod and left.

At a few minutes past six, there was a knock at the door. I concealed myself in the pantry, leaving the door open a crack, and Wilson let in his visitor. As they were in the parlour I could not hear the exact words of their conversation, but I could detect the rise and fall of voices, the jocular tone to begin with, then the wheedling, then something more threatening, before the visitor decided to cut his losses and leave – I daresay Wilson's boxer's build made him think better of pursuing the matter too hard. Wilson came into the kitchen, took off his cravat and waistcoat to reveal a much plainer and less memorable outfit, and we left by the back door, poking our noses out into Norton Street just in time to see Mr Leonard Benson – for that was the name he had given Wilson – turn the corner into Carburton Street.

We followed him into Portland Road, taking care to walk one on either side of the street, and on into Great Portland Street. We all three negotiated Oxford Street, and then our quarry turned left into Princes Street. I signalled to Wilson to take the same turning, while I carried on to Hanover Street, reasoning that I would see Benson passing me in Hanover Square. He continued heading south, pausing occasionally to tip his hat at one ladybird or another, or to peer into the windows of the fine shops on Old Bond Street. Behind us, the bell of St George's marked half-past seven, and Benson picked up his pace, crossing Piccadilly and dropping down into St James's Street before stopping outside a fine building on the left. White's, a gentlemen's club with Tory sympathies, was recognisable thanks to its large bow window giving out onto the street. This was the public face of the club; the sizeable gaming and billiards rooms for which it was famous were, I understood, tucked away at the back. Wilson and I turned purposefully into Bennet Street, and then doubled back on ourselves to stand in the shadows and watch Benson. I nudged Wilson.

"You've heard of Beau Brummell, the dandy?" I asked. He nodded. "He used to sit in that big bow window, and other gentlemen would crowd outside to see what he was wearing and then rush home to put on a similar costume. Although I doubt that he ever wore his sister's petticoat round his neck." Wilson blushed.

Benson was looking up at the first floor windows of the building, and after a few minutes he nodded to someone. He then sauntered away and waited further down the street, passing the time by taking a little snuff. As we all waited, a gig came bowling up the street and pulled to a halt outside White's. A young man jumped out, handing the reins to his groom. Another man coming down the steps from White's spotted him and called out, "Knapton, my fine fellow! The tables are a little rich for you tonight – keep your wits about you, if you have any!" He then laughed and walked off down the street.

So that was the Right Honourable George Knapton – perhaps here to turn his mother's missing jewels into wagers after all. But I was not the only one to take notice of Knapton's arrival. Benson gave a low whistle, and when Knapton turned in his direction, he gave a mock bow and tipped his hat at the gentleman. Knapton did not seem equally pleased to see Benson; he glanced at his groom, then frowned and hurried up the steps into the club.

About ten minutes later, a man came out of White's; from his dress, a servant rather than a member. He glanced up and down the street, and walked quickly to meet Benson. The two spoke quietly for a moment, and then the servant handed Benson a package, about the size of a book, wrapped in brown paper. He scurried back into the club while Benson turned the package over in his hands, smiled to himself and strolled off down the street. Once he had gone round the corner into Pall Mall, we followed. We saw him hail a cab, and so we did likewise, instructing the jarvey to pursue him at a discreet distance.

We headed into Pall Mall East, trotted steadily along the Strand, past the two churches, and then continued into Fleet Street. Just as Ludgate Hill rose before us, Benson's cab turned left into the maze of streets between Fleet Street and Holborn. I rapped on the roof of our cab and we stopped – we would be too obvious if we followed him further. While I paid, I told Wilson to run on ahead and keep pace with Benson. When I caught up with Wilson, he was standing open-mouthed.

"You'll never guess where he's gone, sir," he said, pointing down a street.

I followed his astonished gaze, and found myself looking at the twenty-foot high wall and stone archways that signified the entrance to the Fleet, one of London's three prisons for debtors.

"He just went up to the door, knocked, and went in," said Wilson disbelievingly.

"Then that is what we shall do," I said, and led Wilson up the street. The three stone arches in the centre of the wall were for show; the real entrance was off to one side, with a heavy wooden and studded door. I banged on it, and a gatekeeper scraped back the viewing panel.

"Your business?" he growled.

"I am a constable, and I should like to know more about the man who just entered."

"And I should say that's none of your business," said the gatekeeper.

Wilson stiffened at my side, but I put up a hand. In debtors' prisons, the only currency is, well, currency. "I daresay that Mr Conant, the magistrate on whose orders I act, would permit the payment of a small consideration in exchange for this information."

The gatekeeper thought for a moment, then shut the panel and hauled open the door. He was a filthy creature, such as would never have been tolerated by John Wontner over at Newgate, but standards at the Fleet had dropped when the warden John Eyles became incapacitated through age and deafness, and even though his replacement was now in post, fallen standards are much harder to raise than those that have been maintained all along. The gatekeeper held out a grubby paw, and I handed over a few coins.

"Lenny Benson, that was," he said, jerking his head over his shoulder.

"An inmate?" I asked.

"Once upon a time, and I daresay will be again," said the gatekeeper, with what might have been a chuckle before it ended in a cough, "but not right now, no."

"So he is visiting someone?"

"Oh, we welcome visitors, we do," said the gatekeeper with a leer.

"Indeed," I said. "Constable Wilson, this fine prison has the reputation for being the biggest bawdy-house in London." I turned back to the gatekeeper. "So is Mr Benson that kind of visitor?"

"Oh no," said the man hurriedly, shaking his head. "He's here, as you might say, on business." His eyes strayed to the pocket from which I had taken the coins I had already paid him. "Comes here every evening about this time, to report on the day's business."

I let my fingers play with some coins in my pocket, as though considering the matter. "And to whom does he make these daily reports?"

The gatekeeper looked over his shoulder, then back at my pocket and licked his lips. I could almost hear him making his decision.

"To his master, of course," he said. I took my empty hand out of my pocket. He thought for a moment more, then shook his head and pushed the door closed in our faces. Wilson looked at me in surprise.

"So we know we're dealing with someone substantial," I said as we walked away from the prison. "Someone with eyes and ears everywhere."

CHAPTER TWENTY-TWO

The work of a deranged mind

THURSDAY 8TH SEPTEMBER 1825

Mr Conant stood at his window looking back at me, his spectacles in his hand and a puzzled frown on his face. "Are you telling me, constable, that you believe that the man running these schemes is already in gaol? That he is organising it all from inside the Fleet?"

"Indeed, sir, yes," I said.

He shook his head disbelievingly. "Remind me, Sam, about the ludicrous legal position of debtors in this city."

"If a man is in debt, sir, the court will order him into the Fleet – or the King's Bench or the Marshalsea – and there he will remain until his debtors are satisfied."

"What madman dreamt up such a situation?" asked the magistrate. "So as a punishment for being in debt, a man will be removed from any opportunity to make his living, thus making repayment of his debts even more unlikely. And I understand, and you will have heard the same, I am sure, that some will lay themselves open to charges of debt in order, in effect, to commit themselves to prison to escape their debtors – for the law states that while a man is in prison for debt, his property cannot be seized." Again he shook his head. "The whole thing is the work of a deranged mind."

I had to agree. "And the Fleet would be perfect for the requirements of such a man. It is the most comfortable and modern of London's gaols, especially for those who can afford the higher commitment fee and the chamber rent to reside on the Master's side. And I have no doubt that our man will also have paid to be granted liberty of the rules."

"Which means that he is allowed outside the gaol?"

"Yes: within the precincts known as the rules – in short, Ludgate Hill, the Old Bailey, Fleet Lane, and part of Fleet Street and Farringdon Street. Enough to stretch his legs and to fool himself that he is a free man. He has no need to go any further, as he has runners for that. And – if what I think is correct – he will actually prefer to stay within the rules, where he can have a bodyguard in attendance all the time. He will have made plenty of enemies over the years, I am sure, and he would rather not meet any of them in a dark alleyway."

Conant returned to his table and sat down. "If this is the case, Sam, it presents us with something of a conundrum. I am a diligent magistrate and you a determined constable, but even we cannot send to prison a man who is already there."

"He's right of course, your Mr Conant," said Martha that evening as we sat together after dinner. "Do you carry pebbles around in your boots, Samuel Plank – the darning I have to do on your stockings!" She tutted as she took another item from her mending basket. "But if this dreadful man is clever enough to hide away in prison, you will have to be even cleverer."

"Even cleverer?" I looked across at her as she searched for some matching yarn. "What do you mean?"

"Well, a punishment is only a punishment if it's something you don't want, isn't it?" she asked. I nodded. "And it seems that this fellow is perfectly happy to be in prison, so it's not really any form of punishment for him. So..." she looked up at me.

"So I need to think of something that would be a punishment for him – something he would loathe."

"That's it. Do you know much about him?"

I shook my head. "The gatekeeper was too frightened to tell me a name. I did wonder whether he was anything like Mr Gardner."

Martha paused in her darning and looked at me. "Your Mr Gardner, from the Marshalsea? But he'd be long dead by now, surely."

"Oh, I don't think it's him, Mar – he was at heart a kind man, and I'm not at all convinced that the man in the Fleet has any kindness in him at all."

Martha peered closely at the stocking she was holding. "Well, if you ask me, Sam…" she waited.

"Which of course I do," I finished as always, and we both laughed – people often underestimate the warmth that comes from the shared humour of a long marriage.

"If you ask me, you need to learn more about this man – only then will you be able to devise a punishment to fit him." She tied a careful knot in a length of yarn. "The Fleet is open to visitors, you said?"

"Aye: the gates open at five o'clock in the morning during the summer, and stay open until ten at night. Anyone can come and go freely, if sober."

"Well, there you are, then. Get someone on the inside who can report back to you about this man. What about Constable Wilson?"

CHAPTER TWENTY-THREE

Sam's apprenticeship

THURSDAY 8TH SEPTEMBER 1825

L ater that evening Martha tidied the kitchen while I had a wash, and then we went to bed. She was soon asleep, her soft warmth rising and falling slowly beside me, but I lay there for some time, my mind full of recollections. Wilson's imminent visit to the Fleet, and his coming indoctrination into the ways of swell men and scoundrels, had awoken memories that I had thought long buried.

My knowledge of life in a debtors' prison was more than just theoretical. When I was fourteen, my father's lighter had been rammed by another vessel and sank to the bot-

tom of the river. In order to buy another – for a lighterman without a boat will soon starve – he borrowed
money from several people, handing over IOUs in good
faith. But times were hard on the river, and when he
could not meet his vowels, he was sent to the Marshalsea
prison in Southwark – and my mother, sister and I went
with him. We were in there for only seven months, as
my mother was able to earn money by doing laundry and
mending for other prisoners, putting aside every coin
that she could to satisfy my father's creditors, and I, well,
I contributed to the family coffers too. But it was the
memory of how I did it that haunted me now.

My parents had been very modern in their outlook.
Unschooled themselves, although my father managed to
scrape by with basic letters and numbers, they were determined that their two sons would escape the alleyways
of Wapping and earn a living that didn't involve the all-
pervading stench of river water. They presented each of
us to the local charity school when we turned eight; Joe
went for a couple of years but once he knew his letters
and numbers well enough to read the labels on bundles of
cargo and calculate the profit on a sale, he stopped going.
I, on the other hand, could not get enough of what the
schoolmasters were telling me. I was fascinated by the
realisation that, with words, I had access to all the
knowledge in the world. I had a particular aptitude for
numbers, often winning pennies from school-friends by

doing sums more quickly in my head than they could do on a slate, but it was the stories, especially of history, that captured me. Not that I was an angel, not by any means – I had my fair share of beatings for mischief and cheek. But when my father was sent to the Marshalsea, I am sorry to say that my hottest tears were shed for the loss of my schooling.

I can still remember the day I first met Mr Gardner. We had been in the Marshalsea for about a month, so it would have been November 1794. As usual, I woke early, shivering with cold from another night spent on a thin pad of horsehair laid straight onto the stone floor. I tried not to think about the likelihood of that thin pad being infested with lice, as even the idea of it made my skin crawl and itch. I had begged to be allowed to bring my mattress from home, but that – along with the bed beneath it and the rest of our meagre furniture – had been sold in increasingly desperate attempts to pay off our father's loans. For the time being, we could just about afford, thanks to the goodwill of our few friends back in Wapping and my mother's labour, to keep a room to ourselves in the prison by buying out the other prisoner who had been allocated to it as well, but I knew that the day could not be far off when we would be forced to take in a chum.

I stood up and dressed quickly, shaking out my clothes to make sure that no rats had nested in them overnight.

My parents slept on, and I looked across at the old petticoat that my older sister Lizzie – sixteen and nothing but a torment to me – had strung up across a corner of the room to give herself some privacy as she slept on her mattress, but there was no sound or movement from any of them and so I carefully opened the door and made my way down the narrow wooden staircase and out of the barracks into the yard.

No-one was around, which was a rare occurrence for the debtors' side of the Marshalsea, with hundreds of people squeezed into the rooms making up its eight houses. The gate was still closed – it wouldn't open officially until eight o'clock – but the keeper knew me and let me out. Clutched in my pocket were the two pennies my mother had given me the night before; when we first arrived she had given me five pennies every evening, then three, but still our funds dwindled.

When I ducked back into the prison ten minutes later with a bag of bread ends in my hand, someone tapped me on the shoulder. I recognised Dumb Tom, a mute who ran errands for other prisoners – very busy he was too, as everyone knew that no matter what he saw, he couldn't tell anyone about it. He beckoned me to follow, putting a finger to his own useless lips to indicate that we should both stay silent, and darted back towards the barracks. He led me up the left-most staircase to the top floor, where the most favoured rooms were, and on one of them he knocked quietly, three times quickly then once more. The door opened, Tom waved me in, and the door closed behind me. Tom had gone.

"So you're the Plank boy," said a man leaning back in an armchair. An armchair! "Come close so that I can see you." I walked towards him, past two other men sitting at a table with books open in front of them. Ledgers, they looked like. I realised that although the room looked like any of the others from the outside, it was in fact three whole rooms knocked into one, with the dividing walls removed. "You're small for fourteen, but then I daresay you're not getting much to eat these days. Eh, boy?"

"No, sir," I said, conscious of the bag of bread in my hand, and unable to take my eyes off the plate of food sitting seemingly abandoned on the table next to the man's chair.

He followed my gaze and held out the plate. "Go on: help yourself." I hesitated; no-one in the Marshalsea gave away anything for nothing. "Go on – I'll just give it to the rats if you don't want it." I reached out and took a pasty, chewing it slowly while looking at my benefactor. He was about the age of my father, but more fleshy and much better dressed. His coat, although obviously not new, was made of sturdy material and fitted him well around the shoulders, while his white stock and stockings were freshly laundered – perhaps my own mother had done them. I finished the pasty and waited. The man in the chair steepled his hands in front of him.

"Eighteen multiplied by nine?" he asked suddenly.

I stared at him, and looked round at the two men who were not paying us any attention at all.

"Eighteen multiplied by nine?" he repeated.

"One hundred and sixty-two," I replied.

"One hundred and fifty divided by nineteen?"

"Between seven and eight."

"Nearer to seven or nearer to eight?"

"Much nearer to eight."

"If I start out with ten guineas and I wager two guineas on six cockfights one after the other, doubling my stake if I win and losing it if I lose, and I win four and lose two, what do I go home with?"

"A whore!" called out one of the men at the table, but my questioner ignored him, studying my face as I worked on the calculation.

"Fourteen guineas," I said eventually.

The man nodded. "Does it matter in what order my wins and losses come?"

"No," I said. "There aren't enough losses for it to matter – although with more losses you could lose all your money before starting to win."

The man nodded, turning down his lips thoughtfully. "Well, Mr Plank, it seems that Mr Harrison was right.

He's been watching you in the tap room, helping the toppers with their card-games when they're too drunk to add up, and he said you had a natural facility with numbers. I could use a lad like you, if you're keen to learn and willing to work."

"What sort of work, sir?" I asked.

"I have lots of interests, Mr Plank, both here in the Marshalsea and beyond. Keeping track of it all is a business in itself, as you can see." He waved his hand towards the two men at the table. So they were ledgers. "Written records are one thing, but I need someone quick-witted, who can tell instinctively whether he's been short-changed or over-charged, who can work out interest on a loan on the doorstep – and even better if they can move around unnoticed. Is that someone you, Mr Plank? My work is well-paid, as you can see." His sweeping arm gesture managed to take in the large chamber with proper curtains, the fire in the grate, the two men working diligently to his orders, his own fine clothes and well-fed body, as well as hinting at much more outside the prison walls.

I savoured the last traces of pasty in my mouth and made up my mind. "Yes, sir. Without a doubt, sir."

And so it had begun. The look of amazement and relief on my mother's face as I handed over five shillings at the end of my first week of working for Mr Gardner was all the encouragement I needed. My father said nothing;

we couldn't afford the fee for him to go outside the prison walls, as the rest of us could, and so he grew quieter and more withdrawn. Over the next months I became more sure of myself, arrogant even. Word spread quickly that I was one of Gardner's men, and the other prisoners took care to treat me with respect, pressing themselves into the wall as I passed. Even those who sat on the debtors' committee didn't dare say anything against me; others would be fined for making noise after midnight or singing obscene songs or throwing filthy water out of the window of their room, but not me – even though I did all of that and more. In short, I was well on my way to becoming a thug.

And then my father fell ill. As I have said, his spirit was low – and I agree with Martha that when the mind is troubled, the body too becomes prey to all manner of complaints. I daresay a medical man might have proffered a different diagnosis, but my mother knew her husband.

"He misses the river," she would say, sitting beside him and stroking his hand as he slept fitfully. "At night, his arms move as though he's paddling."

One day, as I reluctantly took my turn watching over him, I was sitting impatiently by the bed, counting the seconds until my sister returned and I could get on with my proper business. I was gazing out of the window, so I did not see him staring at me – and I jumped when he grabbed my arm in a surprisingly strong grip. I had thought that strength – borne of years of steering against the current and hauling bales of cargo – had gone, but no.

"You're on the wrong path, Sam," he said fiercely. "I know you think you're cock of the walk, with your pocket full of coins and all the girls batting their eyes at you. But it's all filthy, Sam: the coins, the girls. All filthy. None of it earned honestly. I've already lost one good boy to it – don't you dare follow him." By now his grip on my arm was hurting, but he did not weaken. "Your mother and me, we taught you right from wrong. If doing right was easy, everyone would do it. It's only for the strong, Sam. Break away while you're still strong enough to take the right path. You feel that?" I nodded mutely. "That's me giving you the last of my strength."

And grown lad that I was, I felt the tears prickling in my eyes. I reached into my pocket for a handkerchief, and pulled out a silk one. I had taken it the night before in payment for a gambling debt from some poor soul in the tap room, and the shame washed over me.

I went to see Gardner that very evening and explained that my father wouldn't last much longer in prison. For-tune had been smiling on me all along; Gardner was a rogue rather than a villain, with a soft heart for a sad story. I worked another month for him, and he gave me more jobs and allowed me to keep a larger proportion of my takings. I stopped spending on grog and skittles, and – ashamed though I was to mix my tainted money with my mother's hard-earned pennies – between us we put aside enough to pay off my father's creditors. I was sent to each of them with the sum owing, and a petition for them to sign. When all were satisfied, I presented the petition to the keeper of the Marshalsea, and my father was released.

We returned to our home in Wapping, now bare and shabby with everything sold. Alarmed by what had happened with Mr Gardner, my parents were keen to get me away from bad influences, and so they boarded me with a cousin of my mother's who lived in Piccadilly. Along with her son I started working as a runner for the magistrates and constables at Great Marlborough Street, and then one day a magistrate caught me reading a note I had been handed, realised I was literate, and suggested that I try life as a constable. My father never worked again, but he lived long enough to see me in my blue uniform and died soon afterwards, with the sounds of his beloved river in his ears.

CHAPTER TWENTY-FOUR

Wilson and the watch

FRIDAY 9TH SEPTEMBER 1825

"Sal says I have to buy her a new petticoat," grumbled Wilson as I checked him over in the back room at Great Marlborough Street. "She says this one has spent so long around my neck that she doesn't want it back. It would have been cheaper to buy a cravat in the first place."

I walked around him, adjusting the shoulders of his coat. "I'll have a word with Mr Neale," I said. "I daresay a little petty cash can be found – although quite how he will account for a new petticoat in the office-keeper's books, I wouldn't like to guess. Now, put on the hat and let's have a good look at you."

Jem Butler's gentleman never did return for his silk top hat and the jarvey was planning to take it to a pawnbroker, but he had agreed to let us use it a while longer.

I looked at Wilson thoughtfully. "All you're missing is this." I drew out my watch and unclipped it. Wilson took it wordlessly and turned it over in his hand. "It's not worth a great deal in money terms, but Mrs Plank gave it to me and I treasure it for that." He nodded and slipped it into his pocket. "Now you look the part. Are you ready?"

Wilson swallowed and nodded.

"Can you remember everything we worked out?"

Wilson started to count on his fingers. "One: leave the police office in a temper, slamming the door."

"Because?"

"Because if anyone has seen me with you in the past and is following us, they will think that we've had a falling out."

I nodded, thinking back to the man in the canary waistcoat – there he was in Langham Place, and near the Turk's Head, and at the investment meeting in the Crown and Anchor. Those who make a living from deceiving others are usually well schooled in observing faces.

Wilson continued. "Two: go to the Turk's Head and wait for one of the magpies to come in."

"And how will you recognise him?"

"He will look even more ridiculous than I do," said Wilson with some warmth. "Three: wait for him to approach me, or, if he does not, approach him myself."

"But not too keenly," I reminded him, "otherwise he will scent a rat. You must be casual, almost as though it is a game – remember, you are a young man on the make, disillusioned with life as a police officer, recently come into a little money, and now keen for some sport at the expense of others. If he knows about Benson's visit the other evening, just say that you've thought better of the offer you refused before. I suspect that the lure of corrupting a constable will be irresistible. Four?"

"Four: try to remember everything he tells me, but..." he held up a hand as I was about to interrupt, "but do not write anything down until I am alone."

"Very good: the notebook would give you away in an instant."

"And five: hail a cab to go just around the corner and then walk back to your house by an indirect route."

"If you are not there by," I felt in my pocket and had a moment's panic until I remembered. "Show me the watch." He did. "If you are not at my house by eight o'clock, I shall come to the Turk's Head myself to find you."

"Was that quarter past or half past the hour?" I said to Martha as the church bells tolled.

"Goodness me, you're on pins and needles this evening, Sam," she said, lifting the lid on a pot on the range and sniffing the contents. "Half-past, and he'll be here as soon as he can. Ah – I told you so." She went to the back door and opened it, and Wilson ducked in, removing his hat.

"Sit, sit." Martha all but pushed Wilson down onto the bench. "And you," she turned to look at me, "no questions until he's had something to eat. Pour him a drink – unless you're a trifle disguised already?" She peered at Wilson.

"No, not me," he said, shaking his head solemnly. "I had a pot or two to play the part, but I can hold my liquor." He took the plate of stew that Martha held out to him, and fell on it. She watched him with satisfaction.

When he had cleaned the plate twice over, Wilson sat back and stretched out his legs.

"Well?" I said, rather impatiently I am afraid. "Did you meet anyone?"

Wilson nodded. "It went off just as you said. I sat at a table in the drinking parlour, looking bored, and I had an idea: if I fiddled with a pair of dice, it would show that I enjoyed a wager."

Martha laughed. "Well, I can tell he's one of yours, Sam."

Wilson looked pleased, and sat more upright to continue his tale. "This swell came in, just as you said he would, and spotted me right off. He sat down with me, all friendly, and we got to talking – well, he talked and I listened. Jonas Holden, he said his name was, and he certainly had the patter. At first, I think he was going to try to get me to invest – it was like at that meeting, all the talk about an opportunity that I had to grab. But I let slip that I had been a constable but was sick of it, and that I quite fancied doing what he was doing, and that seemed to tickle him. I asked him who he worked for, but he was no whiddler and kept his mouth shut about that."

"So what next?" I asked. "Are you to meet him again?"

Wilson smiled broadly. "Better than that, sir. Tomorrow I'm meeting Mr Holden again – and, if he's got permission by then, he's taking me to meet his chief."

Martha's hand went to her mouth, and I knew what she was thinking, for I was thinking the same myself. As far as Wilson was concerned, we were trying to trap a swindler – but Martha and I both suspected that we were hunting a much more ruthless man.

CHAPTER TWENTY-FIVE

Martha takes charge

SATURDAY 10TH SEPTEMBER 1825

The morning after Wilson's proposed meeting with Holden, the first rays of light were just showing and I was already awake, having barely slept at all, when I heard a soft knock at the back door. I shrugged a jacket over my nightshirt, went downstairs and opened the door, staggering backwards as Wilson fell onto me. I grasped him under the arms and half-walked, half-dragged him to a chair. As I took my hands away, I saw in the faint dawn that they were bloodied. Wilson slumped forwards with a groan.

"Martha!" I called. "Come quickly!"

I am always bemused when men – usually lifelong bachelors, to be sure – refer to women as the weaker sex. For my money, in a crisis there is no man that can match a woman for decisiveness and quick thinking. On Martha's directions, between us we hauled Wilson into my large armchair, removed his boots and propped his legs up on another chair. As I struggled to undo the buttons of his torn and stained shirt she elbowed me aside and sliced through the material with her sharpest kitchen knife, taking care to peel away the fabric carefully and gently.

"Light the lamp," she instructed me, "and hold it so that I can check for any wounds." Wilson moaned again. "No need to worry now, William," she said softly. "You're safe, and Martha will take care of you."

She worked her way methodically around Wilson's torso, indicating to me to lean him forward and support him on my shoulder while she inspected his back. She then took hold of each of his arms in turn, first looking at them and then working her hands along them. As she pressed his left hand, he winced and gasped.

"A basin of warm water, please, Sam, and that cloth drying on the rack in the kitchen," she said. I was glad of something to do. When I returned with what she wanted, she took the cloth, dipped it in the water and expertly cleaned the blood from Wilson's skin. He opened his eyes and looked at her, and a tear worked its way down his cheek. I looked away, and when I looked back, Martha had wiped that away too.

While Martha turned her back, I pulled off Wilson's trousers and helped him into my spare nightshirt – it looked comically short on him, but none of us was in the mood for laughing. We settled him back into the chair, put a cushion behind his head and two blankets over him, and he was asleep in seconds. Martha and I went to our bedroom to dress ourselves and I pushed the door to so as not to disturb Wilson, although I suspected that he would sleep through a cavalry charge. Martha said nothing, but I could see her anger in the bright spots of colour high on her cheeks, and in the way she jabbed the pins into her hair. When we were both dressed we returned to the kitchen, first checking that Wilson was still asleep in his chair.

Martha went to the range as though to start our usual breakfast, but instead of moving pots and laying the table she just stood with her back to me. I quietly put a hand on her shoulder, and she turned her head to lay her cheek on it.

"Did we send him to that, Sam?" she asked quietly.

I wanted to reassure her but I couldn't. To say no would be a lie. Martha and I had devised our clever plan, and now Wilson had paid the price for it being not quite clever enough.

We stood in silence for some minutes. Then Martha took a breath, smoothed down her apron, and turned to face me.

"First of all, we must send a message to William's mother; she will be worried about him by now. Not the truth, of course – time enough for that later – just say that he is helping you with something and will be home tomorrow evening. The worst of the swelling will have gone by then." I nodded.

Once the note was written, I went into the street and beckoned to a lad standing at the corner. The smart ones know to stay near police officers and lawyers, who always have need of urgent deliveries. I handed him the note and told him the address.

Back in the kitchen, Martha was sitting at the table with the teapot in front of her and two cups standing ready.

"He was lucky, Sam – such a beating might have crippled a less robust man. His ribs are bruised, maybe one or two cracked. Most of the blood is from a wound on the back of his head – probably hit it on the ground as he went down – and from a split lip. Two broken fingers on his left hand. When we've had this tea and he's properly asleep, I'll bind them so that they mend straight."

"But nothing from a weapon? A knife?"

She shook her head. "Mercifully, no."

"So a warning, then," I said. "Meant to frighten rather than to kill."

Wilson slept all day; at about midday Martha went in with a bowl of broth and sat on a low stool beside him, spoon-feeding him like a child. Later I went in with a pot so that he could relieve himself. Martha stayed my hand as I was about to empty the pot outside and peered into it.

"No blood," she said approvingly. "If they had wounded him inside, there would be blood."

We were just sitting down to our dinner at about six when we heard shuffling steps and Wilson appeared in the doorway of the kitchen, his hair on end and his poor face all misshapen, clutching the blankets around him like a shawl.

"That smells good," he said thickly.

I held out a chair for him, and Martha took another plate from the dresser and filled it. Before placing it in front of Wilson, she cut up the larger pieces of meat and handed him a spoon. He looked down at his bound fingers in surprise, and then started to eat.

"Your mother knows that you're staying with us for tonight," said Martha conversationally. "We didn't mention your – accident."

Wilson nodded as he chewed.

I finished my own dinner and sat back in my chair. Wilson emptied his plate; wordlessly Martha took it from him and refilled it, and we both watched him finish his second helping.

"No damage to your stomach, then," I said.

Wilson tried to smile and winced instead. "Thank you, Mrs Plank," he said as he put his spoon down. "And for earlier. Both of you. I couldn't go home looking like that – my mum's not a strong woman."

Martha leaned over and patted Wilson's good hand. "You did the right thing, William, coming here. You're not the first beaten man I've had to tidy up." She tilted her head at me and winked at Wilson. "Sam was waiting up for you anyway."

"Were you, sir?" asked Wilson, looking pleased.

"Well, not waiting for you, exactly, just awake early wondering about our man in the Fleet," I said quickly. I shot Martha a look, and she smiled innocently back at me.

"I can tell you more about him, if you like," said Wilson.

"So you did meet him, then? Holden took you to him?"

Wilson nodded. "You were right about him. He wanted to know all about my work as a constable – how long I had done it for, why I wanted to leave, who I worked with. I didn't mention any names, but I did tell him that I worked out of Great Marlborough Street, in case any of his men had reported seeing me there."

I nodded approvingly. "What was he like?"

"Tall, nearly as tall as me. Well-built. Pale skin, red hair going grey. A scar here," Wilson indicated his left cheek, "and several on the back of his right hand."

My blood chilled. But surely not, after all these years? "And as a man?" I asked. "What was he like as a man?"

Wilson considered. "Friendly, talkative – but I felt that he was watching and listening to me more closely than other men do. Remembering everything."

"The mark of a good scoundrel," I commented. "Always know more about your mark than he knows about you." I remembered my own visits to Mr Gardner's room in the Marshalsea. "Where in the Fleet is he?"

"In the main building," replied Wilson, drawing a plan on the table with his forefinger as he spoke, "then two flights up the main staircase, along a gallery to the end."

"As I thought: one of the chapel chambers. He's doing well for himself, then – they're the largest rooms in the prison."

"You should have seen it, sir – better decked out than my mum's place!" He shook his head. "He had all his sticks with him: two armchairs, fine hangings on the walls, rugs on the floor."

"And did you discuss his kind offer?"

"Of working for him?" I nodded. "As I say, he spent quite a while asking about why I wanted to leave my current work, and what had turned me against it. He suggested that, with my recent good fortune – I suppose Benson or Holden had told him all about it – I might prefer simply to invest. But I told him that I knew that the clever money was to be made through signing up other subscribers, and that was what I wanted to do."

"Did he bite?"

"Not straight away, no. He said that I had to prove myself, that I could work alongside one of the other magpies for a month or two, watching and learning. An apprenticeship, he called it – unpaid, of course."

"Of course," I repeated.

"I don't think he quite trusted me, and wants me to show my bona fides before he gives me my own book, as he called it."

"But why did he beat you, William?" asked Martha.

"He thought I had stolen something," said Wilson. "On a table in his cell there was a book lying open, and he saw me notice it. After I'd left and was on my way back down to the prison courtyard, three of his men came chasing after me and hauled me back in front of him. The book had gone, apparently, and they thought I had it. I said I didn't, but he told them to search me. I resisted, and, well, you can see what happened."

A distant memory came back to me. "Your fingers, Wilson – what happened there?"

Wilson held up his hand and contemplated them. "He did that, himself. He seemed to enjoy it, too."

Martha put a hand over her mouth. "Sam…" she said, looking at me, and I nodded.

Wilson continued. "I suppose he thought to make me hand over the book, but even he had to admit in the end that I didn't have it, and so they let me go."

"God help whoever did take it," breathed Martha.

"Oh, it was me," said Wilson. "When you've arrested a few pickpockets, Mrs Plank, you learn the best places to conceal things."

"Well!" said Martha, laughing. "So what did you do with it?"

"When I took it I stuffed it down the back of my trousers, under my jacket. And when I heard them running after me I hid it behind a bench in the prison yard. I collected it on my way out and brought it back here." He looked from me to Martha and we both shook our heads. "Well, I had it with me, I know that."

"Maybe you dropped it when you collapsed on me," I suggested. I went to the back door and opened it; sure enough, lying on the ground just outside was a fair-sized book with a shabby cover. I picked it up and put it on the table.

"But why on earth did you take such a risk just for a book?" asked Martha in astonishment.

"Not just a book, Mrs Plank," said Wilson, pushing it towards me and opening it.

I looked down at the pages in front of me. "No, not just a book," I agreed. "A ledger. A ledger of accounts."

Wilson and I wanted to start work on the ledger straight away but Martha was having none of it.

"You're recovering from a bad beating," she said nodding at Wilson, "and you barely slept a wink last night," this directed at me, "so that book can wait until morning. William, we'll push together the armchairs and line them with cushions and blankets, and you'll be as snug as anything for tonight." I could tell from her voice and from the efficient way she set about making a bed for Wilson that there was no point disagreeing with her. Wilson was starting to look tired again anyway, and was happy to be tucked into his blankets like a little boy. Just as I turned to go upstairs, he suddenly remembered something.

"Your watch, sir," he said. "It's still in the pocket of my waistcoat." I retrieved the waistcoat from the kitchen chair where Martha had laid it and handed it to him. He felt in the pocket and pulled out the watch, and turned to me with a stricken look on his face. "Oh! It must have been when I was on the ground and they were kicking me. I tried to protect it, but..." and he held out the watch to me. There was an obvious dent in the case. I opened it carefully, then showed it to Wilson.

"See? Still going. Just like you: a bit bruised, a bit battered, but still working." Wilson still looked mortified. I smiled at him. "In fact, I think it's improved it. Now, whenever I look at my watch, I shall be reminded of the fine, brave work you did. It will make me proud."

Back in the kitchen, Martha was tidying away the last of the dinner things. I showed her the watch, and she kissed me on the cheek.

"Why did you do that?" I asked.

"Because you, Samuel Plank, have a kind heart," she replied. "And because I saw your face when William was describing the man in the Fleet. Red hair. Likes breaking fingers. It must be him." I nodded. "Oh Sam," she said sadly, and snaked her arm around my waist. "Oh Sam."

Perhaps not unexpectedly, my dreams that night took me right back to where it had started. The twisting alleyways of Wapping, and my own home a stone's throw from Execution Dock where we children gathered, fascinated and terrified, to watch the hangings of pirates sentenced by the Admiralty Court. The constant noise, with ships coming up the Thames at all hours, riding on the tides, and the lightermen – my father among them – dextrously manoeuvring their flat-bottomed barges to carry goods between ship and shore. The smells of cargo from far-off lands mixed with the stench of whatever was tossed into the river and eventually washed up for the scavengers and mudlarks to pick through. Like the other river-rats, as we called ourselves, I spent my early years running through these alleyways, catching a swipe around the ear here and a scolding there for whatever petty mischief amused us that day. Most of us, by the time we were ten, were well on the way to becoming men; for myself, I was working alongside my father – not yet tall or strong enough to pilot the lighter, but certainly able to wield a cargo hook, and push other boats away with my feet to clear our passage. Joseph should have been with us too, but by then, he had already chosen a different path.

Joseph was my elder brother, by just over two years. There had been a sister between us but she failed to thrive, and from the beginning we two boys were inseparable. Everywhere Joe went I would toddle after him, and my mother, busy taking in washing, was happy to see it. He was as fair and handsome as I am dark and plain, but in the body we were obviously brothers, with the same compact build and the same determination – what Martha likes to call my bull-headed stubbornness. But when I was nine and Joe eleven, he fell in with a bad crowd.

There was a gang of lads who would wait outside the local taverns, knowing that sailors who had been at sea for months would quickly find their way to the grog and the women, over-indulge in both, and then be ripe for robbing of handkerchiefs and any leftover coins on their way back to their ships. Some of the sailors would cut up rough, and so the gang started to arm themselves, carrying first sticks and then knives – sometimes the vicious gutting knives used by their own mothers. Organising all of this, and overseeing their maturing into a proper band of thieves and villains, was a tall, thin, quick and vicious lad called George Macintosh, but known to everyone as Georgie Mac. He and his family had come down from Scotland when Georgie was a baby, for his father to find work on the river, but both parents had quickly succumbed to fever and young Georgie soon learned to live on his wits. One of his favoured methods for punishing those who crossed him was to grab their hand and, one by one, pull the fingers back until they broke. I saw it once myself and the cracking sound and the accompanying howls of his victim made my stomach heave, but Georgie simply smiled. His angelic red curls concealed a mind that was twisted and wicked but could charm the birds from the trees, and soon Joe was under his spell.

We never knew quite what happened, of course – the ship's constables had little interest in a scuffle between an Italian sailor and some local lads, as long as no cargo was in danger. As I heard it, Joe, another boy and Georgie were waiting in an alley for sailors to come stumbling out of the Prospect of Whitby. Georgie spotted an Italian and gave the wink to the others. But he chose wrong: the Italian was a long way off drunk, and was able to defend himself. He turned to Georgie, and – so the other lad later told me, but only when I promised not to tell anyone else, so great was his fear – Georgie took hold of my brother and pulled him across so that he was between Georgie and the sailor. My only comfort is that Joe would not have felt much; the sailor's knife was long and sharp, and his aim was true. Georgie left my brother to bleed there on the wet and stinking cobbles, for the tavern-keeper to find when he came out to check the shutters. Joe was three days shy of his twelfth birthday.

CHAPTER TWENTY-SIX

The ledger

SUNDAY 11TH SEPTEMBER 1825

It was nearly nine o'clock by the time we finished, and my head ached with peering at the ledger and working out sums. Martha had sent Wilson home a couple of hours earlier, saying that she and I could work through the last few pages together. Before he had left she had dabbed talcum powder on the worst of his bruises, to spare his mother. I had been about to tease him about wearing not only petticoats but also powder when Martha had caught my eye and shaken her head, so I left it. Now I gathered our sheets of calculations and stacked them up, placing the ledger on top.

"Well," said Martha, stretching her arms above her head and rolling her neck, "that was quite a puzzle. You said he was a clever man."

"Life would be much simpler for constables if only stupid people broke the law," I commented, and earned a mock cuff around the ear for my pains.

"There's a great deal of money there," said Martha, nodding at the ledger.

"I doubt we've found it all," I replied. "After all, this is only one ledger – there might be others. I remember a banker once telling me that criminals often keep two sets of accounts: one for discovery, and one for private." Martha looked crestfallen, so I added quickly, "But we've certainly found enough to make life very difficult for Mr Macintosh, and he cared enough about this ledger to confront Wilson over it."

"You're sure it is him, now that you've read all of that?"

"Oh yes," I replied. "The Scottish connections, Wapping, the smuggling and cargo thefts – all Georgie through and through."

"And you know where to take this?" she asked, yawning and indicating the ledger.

I smiled grimly. "One of the joys of being a constable is that you meet all sorts of interesting people in all manner of useful places. And you don't become as powerful as Georgie Mac without making plenty of enemies along the way. You've heard of honour among thieves?" Martha nodded. "It's a bag of moonshine. Doesn't exist. As soon as word's out that Georgie's on his way down, they'll be falling over themselves to push him further under."

I was just drifting off to sleep, Martha curled around my back, when she nudged me with her knee.

"Sam," she whispered, "I've been thinking about George Macintosh."

"Not for the past half hour, I hope," I mumbled in return.

"Serve you right if I was, Sam Plank," she said, but I could hear the smile in her voice. "No, seriously, Sam, turn around. I've had an idea."

CHAPTER TWENTY-SEVEN

A fitting punishment

MONDAY 12TH SEPTEMBER 1825

"**A**s you know, Constable Wilson has been working with me on the investment matter," I said to Mr Conant. Wilson stood at the door of the magistrate's dining room, reluctant to come any further. I beckoned him in. "Come, Wilson, and show that book to Mr Conant."

Conant took the ledger, and indicated that Wilson should take a seat. I nodded at him, and he did so, gazing around the room. We waited for a few minutes. Eventually the magistrate looked up at us and took off his spectacles.

"But this is a ledger," he said, "showing who has paid into the scheme, and what money has been paid out."

I nodded. "Constable Wilson met with the man running the scheme..."

"In the Fleet?" asked the magistrate in surprise.

"Yes, we decided that as Constable Wilson is still rather less known to London's rogues than I am, it would be safer for him to go. And just as well, too, as it turns out that our man is George Macintosh, with whom I have indeed had prior dealings. So Constable Wilson went in disguise, and after their meeting, he borrowed this book from Mr Macintosh."

Conant raised his eyebrows but said nothing. He leafed through the book again. "And are the names we expected to see in here?"

"They are, yes. Mr Dubois, Mr Wakefield and the Honourable George Knapton are listed as investors, and Mr Dyer is listed as both an investor and a drover."

"A drover?" asked Mr Conant.

"Someone who is told that they can work off their debt by recruiting other subscribers to the scheme," I explained.

"Has the reward tempted out any information about our missing schoolmaster?" asked Conant.

I shook my head. "Nothing yet, sir." The magistrate sighed. "But regarding our current difficulty with Mr Macintosh – how to punish a man who is already in prison – I think this ledger will prove rather helpful. May I?"

I indicated the ledger, and Conant slid it across to me. I turned to the back of it, and pointed to some close-written pages. The magistrate replaced his spectacles and peered at the writing.

"It is a record of where Mr Macintosh has put his money," I explained. "He cannot keep much of it with him in the Fleet, of course, so he has to find safe places for it. And because he is a debtor, he has to arrange his affairs to keep his possessions beyond the reach of his creditors." Conant tutted. "Mrs Plank reminded me that the best way to punish someone is to take away the thing they most value. For most men that is their liberty, but not so for Mr Macintosh, who is living very comfortably in the Fleet, protected day and night from his enemies, and well-cushioned from discomfort by the payment of generous garnish. No, for Mr Macintosh, what he values most is his money – and this ledger tells us where to find that. And Mrs Plank has had a particularly good idea about how to turn his money against him. But we must move swiftly. The loss of this book had already been noticed, and Macintosh's men will be looking for Constable Wilson." I put my hand on Wilson's shoulder.

"Go, then," said Conant. "But perhaps it would be better if we did not mention this meeting to anyone else. I suspect that others might take a dim view of a magistrate authorising punishments beyond the scope of the court – or indeed allowing his men to pursue a scheme cooked up by Mrs Plank." He shook his head in mock regret. "What is the purpose of the finest legal minds in England and their dusty books full of laws if my very own constables and even their wives can see a more sensible way to administer justice?"

CHAPTER TWENTY-EIGHT

Falling from grace

WEDNESDAY 14TH SEPTEMBER 1825

I was waiting outside the bank in Cheapside when Edward Freame came round the corner.

"Constable Plank," he said cheerily, his hand extended. "What a pleasure." And I could tell from his eyes that it was: many men say it, but only a few mean it. "Is this about our poor Mr Dyer?"

"In a manner of speaking, yes," I replied as he ushered me into his bank.

"Good morning, Stevenson," he said to the young clerk who came forward to take our hats and coats. I held onto the package that I had brought with me. "Two teas, if you please – and make one for yourself and one for Mr Harris."

Freame led me to the parlour and indicated that I should sit. "Watch this," he said with a wink. We waited a few minutes, then there was a knock at the door and in came Stevenson with our tea. This time, he made steady progress across the room, put the tray on the table without mishap, and left without tripping or knocking into anything.

"What a difference a few months can make, eh?" asked the banker, handing me a cup. "We've had some breakages along the way, but it's a price worth paying." He sipped at his tea. "So, constable, how can I help you today?"

I explained what we had uncovered about Dyer's involvement with Macintosh's investment scheme, and about the disappearance of the schoolmaster. Freame shook his head sadly and tutted at various points.

"I will pray for his safe return to his family. He has done wrong, to be sure, but he was lured into it by others far more devious and ruthless."

"I agree, Mr Freame, and that is why I am determined to see that Mr Macintosh is punished in the severest way."

The banker stood up in some agitation. "No matter how wicked this man's actions, constable, I cannot assist you in any way if your aim is to have him hang. I am sure I made this clear last time we spoke of it."

I held up my hand to calm him. "Mr Freame, that is not my intention. To be honest, I would struggle to find a lawyer capable of pursuing Mr Macintosh to the scaffold. His schemes have been so cleverly arranged that proving a specific felony would be difficult. Instead, I have decided to fight fire with fire. We know that Mr Macintosh is willing to sacrifice anything – and anyone – at the altar of money." The banker sat down and nodded his agreement. "And so it seems to me that the most suitable punishment for him would be to lose that money." I put my package on my knee and unwrapped it, taking out the ledger and the notes that Martha, Wilson and I had made. "As luck would have it, one of Mr Macintosh's ledgers has come into my possession," the banker's eyes flicked to mine, "and from this we have been able to work out not only how he has been making his money, but also where he has been storing and spending it. I have been through the whole ledger, and determined his main hiding places for his money. Well, I say hiding places, but some are in plain view. And I was wondering, Mr Freame, if you, with your extensive skill as a banker, would be willing to help me take my enquiries to the next stage."

The banker held out his hand for the ledger, and then glanced through it. "This is a meticulous record, constable. Whoever maintains this knows what he is doing." He held out his hand again, without looking up, and I passed across my pages of notes. I let him read in silence.

"You and your two assistants have done an excellent job," he said eventually. I must have looked surprised, because he indicated the notes and said, "Three different hands – two of the same age, and one of a younger person. Bankers learn to look for these things, constable. So: tell me what you need from me."

"As you yourself spotted, Mr Freame, the ledger has been kept to a high, you could say professional, standard. And so I am of the view that a banker is involved."

"I would have to agree with you, constable. The way the ledger is arranged, the symbols used – this all suggests someone who has learned his craft in a bank, yes."

"Would you be able to help me locate this gentleman?"

Freame stood and walked around the room for a few moments, his hand to his mouth in thought. I waited. He came to a halt behind his chair and leaned on it. "Our banking fraternity in London is not small, constable, but neither is it so large that such a man could be unknown. The ledger itself tells us a great deal about him, thankfully." He sat down and opened the ledger on the table in front of us. "Although it covers a period of, what, seven years, it was not started seven years ago: you can see from the uniformity of the entries that it has been compiled more recently."

"Perhaps the records were kept elsewhere, and rationalised into this ledger."

Freame nodded. "My thoughts exactly. And our man is quite young; some of the symbols he uses are modern, and his writing too is modern – less elaborate than that of, say, my own Mr Harris." He reached behind him and pulled out a book of minutes, and showed me a page written by his chief clerk; the script was indeed much more complex and swirling.

"And is the entire ledger in his hand?" I asked. "The back pages as well?"

Freame knew what I was asking. He nodded. "Yes, it is all the work of the same man."

I made another note in my book. "So we are looking for a banker who is still young, yet with enough experience to have organised such a ledger."

Freame put his head on one side and thought for a moment. "My money would be on the son of a recently retired or deceased banker, schooled at his father's knee and now in charge of the show."

I added to my notes. "A young banker who has taken on a criminal as a customer – and who knows exactly what he has taken on. If it were the front of the ledger only, he could claim ignorance, but those pages at the back show that he is fully aware of the fraudulent purpose of the investment scheme." I looked up at Freame. "Why would he become involved, do you think?"

Freame shook his head regretfully. "Few bankers set out to work for criminals," he said. "Certainly the financial rewards can be good, but the dangers are great – and we bankers are not the most daring of people. A man who seeks adventure does not look for it in the banking hall. So I should imagine he fell into it through necessity.

Over-extension of his bank's resources through his own inexperience, I would guess, and along came Mr Macintosh to offer a helping hand – at a price."

"Do you think you could locate such a man?" I asked.

"Drop the right questions in the right ears, you mean?" I nodded. "Yes, I think I could," agreed the banker. "And then what?"

"Well, you could give his name to me, and Mr Conant and I could call him in for a discussion about his situation. Or..."

The banker interrupted me. "If possible, constable, it would be preferable to avoid the official involvement of the magistrates. I believe that none of us is without sin, and everyone is deserving of a second chance. If, as I suspect, the man involved has found himself in financial embarrassment and has taken on this unfortunate business as a way to save his bank and his customers from ruin, I have some sympathy for him – taking on a bank at a young age is a burden few can shoulder without making some mistakes. If I can find our man, and the situation is as I suspect, I propose that I speak to him, tell him what has been discovered, and advise him that the way for him to make amends is to assist you with your enquiries into Mr Macintosh."

"That would be extremely helpful," I said gratefully. "My wife has come up with a rather ingenious way for us to make life unpleasant for Mr Macintosh, and a banker with intimate knowledge of the man's financial arrangements would be of great use."

Freame nodded. "If, on the other hand," he added, "it becomes clear that I am wrong, that our banker is rotten to the core and deliberately chose this path, then I will make him no such offer and will leave him for the courts to deal with."

"Mr Freame, sir, your assistance has been invaluable," I said, closing my notebook and standing. We shook hands in farewell and he walked with me to the door of the bank. While I was putting on my hat and coat, he went to his bank counter and spoke quietly to his senior clerk. And as I left the bank, Freame put a hand on my arm and gave me a purse of coins.

"For Mrs Dyer and her children," he said quietly. Tell her that some of her husband's investments have come good." He shook my hand again. "I'll send word when I have any news."

CHAPTER TWENTY-NINE

Blame it on the blockademen

MONDAY 19TH SEPTEMBER 1825

"Jack Brimer? What do you want with him?" The man behind the counter of the tavern looked at me with undisguised suspicion.

"Nothing to concern you directly," I said. "Or at least not as long as you're sensible about it. I've been told that he drinks in here, and I want to speak to him." I could tell from the man's eyes that he suffered from the same illness as Martha's father: that of the tavern keeper who drinks his profit. "Perhaps something to help you think more clearly?" I nodded towards the bottle of rum on the shelf behind him. "Two."

He reached back for the bottle and poured two tumblers. I put the payment on the counter and he slid the

229

coins into his apron pocket before picking up one of the tumblers and tossing the drink down his throat. I left my tumbler where it was. "All I want to know is where to find Brimer, to catch him on his own. Your name will not be mentioned."

The tavern keeper narrowed his eyes and looked at me – or more specifically, looked at my uniform – and made his decision. "He comes in at Frying Pan Stairs. Used to be a lighterman."

"How will I know him?" The man's eyes flicked to the second tumbler of rum. I waited.

"He wears a purple neckerchief. And his face is pock-marked."

I nodded and pushed the second tumbler towards him.

Frying Pan Stairs were a few streets downstream from my old haunts but it felt familiar all the same. Like all water-men, my father had taught me the litany of the stairs so that I would always know a safe place to land. Tall build-ings – homes, warehouses and shops all jostled in to-gether – shouldered each other out of the way to clear a narrow passage down to the foreshore. Alongside the stairs was, of course, a public house: the first port of call for anyone unfortunate enough to fall into the river and be in need of either a reviving draught or a cool room to await the coroner. I waited at the top of the stairs, folding my arms against the chill breeze drifting off the water, and watched the lightermen settle their boats for the night, calling to each other in their own language of the river. None of them fitted the reluctant description I had been given.

Just as I was considering heading for home and returning the next evening, a lighter nosed its way through the moored boats. At its stern stood a man of about my own age, compact, with the steady footing of a lifelong boatman. He walked along the lighter, jumped easily from it to the dock, and quickly secured its rope to a ring.

I walked down the steps towards him and he looked up at me warily. "Mr Jack Brimer?" I asked, taking note of the scars on his face and the kerchief around his neck.

He folded his arms. "Might be," he replied.

"I am Constable Samuel Plank, acting on behalf of John Conant Esquire, magistrate."

"In that case, I've never heard of this Jack Brimer," he said.

"Mr Brimer," I continued, "I have a proposition for you."

"But a smuggler, Sam," protested Martha as she put my plate before me.

"I know, I know – but it's a sprat to catch a mackerel."

She sat opposite me and watched me eat.

"You would have felt sorry for him, Mar," I said, my mouth full. She frowned and I swallowed before continuing. "His days are numbered, and he knows it. With the blockademen and now the coastguards, smugglers are going to have to think of new ways to ply their trade, and Brimer is too long in the tooth for change. He's been lucky to survive this long."

"So he's decided to make amends for his wicked ways, has he?" she said bitterly.

"Not exactly, no, but Macintosh has been squeezing his profits recently, and Brimer knows a good deal when he sees one. From now on, the brandy that he brings in for Macintosh will be unfortunately seized by the excise men – or at least that's the story he will tell Macintosh. In reality, he will deliver it to Mr Conant's wine merchant. This merchant will sell it, pay the duty on it," Martha nodded approvingly, "take his own profit, and whatever is left will be distributed to various Quaker charities suggested by Mr Freame at the bank."

Martha saw the smile I tried to hide. "Sam Plank, that is just mischief. Giving money from the sale of spirits to Quaker charities – that's like Jesus turning water into wine, but the other way round."

Well, it is not often that I am compared to the Son of God, and certainly not by my own wife.

"So that's the smuggling taken care of," I said. "The more of this plan of yours that I see in action, the more thankful I am that you're on our side."

CHAPTER THIRTY

Pox and property

TUESDAY 4TH OCTOBER 1825

"I thought we agreed that these matters could be left to you, constable," said Mr Conant, looking at me over the top of his spectacles. No matter how often I saw him, and no matter how hard he worked, the pile of papers on his table never seemed to diminish.

I stood with my hands behind my back, and bowed my head in agreement. "We did, sir, yes, and for the most part our – my – plans are proceeding well. But there is one matter in which your assistance would be of great value."

He waved at a chair. "Well, you had better sit down and tell me more." I took a seat.

"It concerns a property in Crawford Street, in Marylebone," I said. "A property owned by Mr Macintosh, according to his own ledger."

"Ah."

"I have a friend who works as a porter at the Smallpox Hospital, at Battle Bridge, and he sometimes overhears the physicians talking. And a few weeks ago two of them were discussing several new cases of smallpox – all in Crawford Street."

Conant shook his head, and glanced at the papers waiting for him on the table. "A terrible fate for those afflicted, of course, but I am afraid that I still cannot see how I can help."

I leaned forward. "You are acquainted with Mr Jeremy Bentham, are you not, sir?" I asked.

Conant nodded. "A most interesting man – some of his ideas are rather queer, but where would we be without such men, thinking the unthinkable?"

"Well, it seems that Mr Bentham's personal physician is Mr Southwood Smith, who is also a physician at the Smallpox Hospital. As such, Mr Smith can authorise the disinfection of the homes of affected patients. And, in extreme cases, recommend the evacuation and demolition of these properties."

"Ah," said the magistrate again. "I begin to follow. You wish me to use my influence with Mr Bentham and his physician to suggest such a course of action for this property in Crawford Street."

I nodded. "It would represent a significant loss to Mr Macintosh."

"And what of the people who live there, in Crawford Street, who will lose their homes?"

"Much as I try, sir, I cannot solve everything," I admitted. "But I have been to this building, and it is a terrible place. Filthy, infested with vermin, public privies. I would not lodge a dog there, sir."

The magistrate nodded, then stood and went to the window, as was his habit when seeking inspiration. I waited. "What we could do, Sam, is box clever," he said, turning to me. "Instead of ordering the building to be demolished, we could issue Mr Macintosh with a recommendation – a strong recommendation mentioning, naturally, my own interest in the matter as a concerned magistrate – for specific improvements to be made, citing the advice of Mr Smith. This would serve both to improve the lot of those living there, and to force Mr Macintosh to spend some money – perhaps a good deal of money – on helping others rather than himself."

I smiled broadly. "I think that would be most fitting, Mr Conant. The best of all worlds, one might say."

"Leave it with me, constable. I dine with Mr Bentham next week, and will talk to him then. Never let it be said that my constables are unimaginative in their interpretation of the scope of their duties."

CHAPTER THIRTY-ONE

The Warmest Welcome

FRIDAY 7TH OCTOBER 1825

From the outside, in the thin afternoon sunshine, the elegant mansion looked just like its neighbours in Golden Square; there was nothing to indicate that this was one of London's most notorious brothels, known as the Aviary. But behind its respectable façade, I knew, there were a dozen rooms, each decorated in a different style to suit all tastes – there was the Grotto for those with a liking for country girls, the Painted Chamber for those with artistic ambitions, the Egyptian Room for those with a taste for the exotic, and many more. In particular, the Aviary was famous for its array of imaginative mechanical and manual items which could gratify the most lascivious appetites. I had been here once or twice before, looking for information about gentlemen who visited its residents, and indeed the maid who opened the door took in my uniform at one glance and stopped acting the coquette as she could tell that I was not here to buy. She left me in a small waiting room, and then returned to ask me to follow her through a sturdy wooden door, concealed behind a draped velvet curtain, and into a parlour beyond.

Sitting in an armchair, a small white dog curled on a cushion at her feet, was Mrs Welcome, referred to by the young bucks as the Warmest Welcome. Her age was hard to tell from her face, powdered and rouged as it was, but from the lines on her throat I judged her to be my contemporary. She did not stand but offered me her hand to kiss, and as I stooped over it, the dog growled.

"Do be quiet, Prinny," she said to the dog. "A gift, unfortunately," she said to me by way of explanation. It was a self-confident woman who could accept a dog from the King, and then name it after him. "And what is it you require, Constable...?"

"Plank, madam – Constable Plank of Great Marlborough Street."

"Oh, do give my regards to Freddie Roe – such a naughty boy!"

"Indeed," I said. If she thought to throw me off my stride with such comments, she was mistaken; I had been dealing with women like her for years. I was certain that if I looked into the past of Mrs Welcome, I would find not only a lack of any Mr Welcome, but also an upbringing as miserable as could be imagined. She would have worked hard to reach the point where she could sit in comfort, a king's dog by her side, and tease a police officer.

"I am looking into the affairs of a man called George Macintosh," I began, watching her for a reaction – but incognitas learn early on how to hide their feelings, and I saw nothing. "We believe that he has been involved in fraudulent behaviour: enticing others to indulge in speculation, by investing money in a venture that does not exist. Many have lost a great deal of money, and some have resorted to desperate measures to escape their losses. One man drank Prussic acid, leaving behind a wife and son."

Mrs Welcome tutted sympathetically, leaning forwards to scratch the dog behind its ear and then feed it a sugared biscuit from the plate at her elbow. "Too sad, constable. But what am I to do? Are you looking for a charitable donation for this poor widow and her fatherless child?"

I smiled. "No, not exactly, although we are hoping to entice Mr Macintosh to make amends for what he has done. Mr Macintosh is the owner of this building." She went to speak, but I held up my hand. "Do not trouble to deny it, madam – we have the proof. And as well as owning the building, he takes a half-share of the profits, with

– I imagine – the other half going to you." She said nothing, which was wise. "With this information, madam, we could charge Mr Macintosh with keeping a brothel and procuring. Or indeed, we could charge you." I stopped for a moment to let that sink in. "You may think that you have the protection of men in power – your magistrate friend Mr Roe for instance, or maybe even…" and I pointed at the dog. "But let me assure you that they will not come to your defence this time. Mr Macintosh is too dangerous for that; no-one will risk being accused of allowing him to flourish."

Mrs Welcome sat back in her chair and looked at me appraisingly. "But you have an offer to make me, constable, otherwise you would not have bothered to come here. You would simply have had me arrested."

I inclined my head in appreciation; I do like clever women. "How often does Mr Macintosh collect his portion?" I asked.

"Every fourth Monday," she said.

"And his last collection was made when?" I asked, opening my notebook.

"We are halfway through this period," she replied.

"I will be confiscating that money from you. Not your portion – you will need that to keep things running as they are, so that no-one suspects anything – but the rest. I will send a constable tomorrow, with a letter signed by a magistrate authorising the collection, and you may keep the letter as a receipt. The constable will write on it the amount he collects. And he will call every three days after that with another letter, to collect Mr Macintosh's portion of whatever money has come in."

"But when Mr Macintosh sends for his money...?"

"We have two weeks before that happens; by then, I am confident that the loss of his takings from you will have quite slipped his mind."

CHAPTER THIRTY-TWO

No boots

SATURDAY 8TH OCTOBER 1825

Martha and I were still in bed the day after my visit to the Aviary when a loud knocking at the door woke us. She opened one eye, gave me a look, and turned over to go back to sleep – the wife of a police officer soon loses her fear of early and late callers. I pulled on a coat over my nightshirt, retrieved a coin from the small pile on the dresser, and opened the front door. A young lad held out a folded note, and I exchanged it for the coin. He touched his forehead and scampered off.

I was just lacing my boots when Martha came out of the bedroom.

"Well?" she said as she fiddled with the pins in her hair, trying to catch the curls.

"They've pulled a body out of the river, and the lighterman who found it is claiming a reward. He reckons it's Dyer."

Martha's hands fell to her sides. "Oh, Sam. I pray for Sarah's sake that he is mistaken."

I generally tried to stay away from the docks, so two visits inside a month was most unusual – and most unwelcome. They have their own Marine Police Force down there, ably assisted by surveyors patrolling the river and ship's constables overseeing the dock gangs, so there is little call for other police officers anyway. For my own part, once I had managed to crawl out of Wapping I had vowed never to return. And when I did have to break that vow occasionally, I tried very hard not to do so at low tide. As a boy I had been used to the stench, but after years away from it my nose had become more sensitive, and now, as I made my way to the Red Cow, the stink revolted me.

The cobbles beneath my feet were slick with river water that dripped from the boots and clothes of the workers who hurried in all directions. Seagulls wheeled and squabbled overhead. I kept an eye out for slops being tossed from windows and doors, and several times had to step over men – and one woman – lying in the gutter already sodden with drink. An old woman sat in a doorway gutting fish, throwing the innards to the cats yowling at the feet. Beside her, a boy of no more than two held out a grubby hand as I passed and I felt in my pocket for a coin. No sooner had I put it into his palm than his grandmother snatched it from him and secreted it under her filthy apron. The boy looked at her in surprise, and his wail of indignation followed me down the alleyway.

I finally reached the doorway of the Red Cow and removed my hat as I entered, pausing for a moment to give my eyes time to adjust to the gloom. The snug was busy, and few paid me any mind as I approached the tavern keeper and asked to see the body.

"And what is your business with it?" he asked, handing two jugs to the girl at his side, pointing to the table that had ordered them, and wiping his hands on his apron. "Are you here to give Thomas his reward?"

"I am Constable Sam Plank, sent here on the orders of John Conant Esquire, magistrate of Great Marlborough Street. I am to identify the body and, if it is the man we seek, to talk to the man who claims that he found it. Thomas?" I took out my notebook.

"Redbridge," said the keeper, leading me down a narrow corridor, past a kitchen filled with steam and chatter, to a heavy wooden door. "A lighterman. He's gone to meet a cargo but he'll be back at noon. Here." He pushed open the door and we looked into a small room, lit only by one small window high in the wall, colder than the rest of the building and once used as a storeroom, I guessed. Taking up most of the space was a simple wooden trestle table, on which lay a shape covered in a cloth. The keeper stood aside and indicated that I should go in.

"Not me," he said. "Once is enough for me to see that." And he went.

I closed the door after him, placed my hat and notebook on a stool in the corner, and approached the table. I paused for a minute, hoping that it would not be the schoolmaster, but knowing in my heart that the lighterman would not have sought the reward if the body did not at least superficially match the description we had circulated. At the head end, I lifted the cloth slowly with two hands, and folded it back onto the chest of the corpse.

Like all lightermen, whether they wanted to or not, my father had recovered several bodies from the river, often with my help, and so this was far from my first experience of looking on a drowned man. And I was grateful – both selfishly and for the sake of Dyer, for it was indeed he – to see that the body had not been long in the water. After days in the water, a body will swell and bloat, and fishes and birds will start to feast on the flesh, but this body, although exhibiting the pale blue tinge common to those who drown, still retained its own shape and proportions. The face was instantly recognisable, with the mouth slightly open and the eyes shut. The smell of the river rose from his clothes.

Just to be thorough, I turned to the other end of the corpse and lifted the sheet here too. I was not surprised to see that the schoolmaster's boots had disappeared. The story would be that the body had been found like that, but I knew that the more likely explanation was that someone had reasoned that a drowned man no longer had need of such sturdy footwear. With them removed, however, I was able to see clearly that one leg was several inches shorter than the other.

Just as I was covering the body again with the sheet, a flash of white caught my eye. Tucked into the pocket of Dyer's coat was a folded sheet of paper – from its condition, it had obviously been put there after the body had been hauled from the water. I opened it and read: "Those who betray the birds end up with the fishes."

I returned to the snug and sat staring at the note. Soon after a nearby church tolled noon, a man entered the tavern and the keeper went to him and pointed me out. The man came to my table and stood before me, twisting his cap in his hands.

"You are Thomas Redbridge?" I asked. He nodded. "You must answer, so that I can write down what you say," I said, indicating my notebook. To those who cannot read or write, the knowledge that their words will be transformed into marks on a page and thus immortalised will often persuade them to be more truthful.

"Yes," he said. "That's me: Thomas Redbridge."

I wrote this down in a slow and exaggerated manner. His eyes watched as the words appeared on the paper.

"And you are a lighterman?"

"A lighterman, yes – like my father afore me."

"And mine," I said.

"Your father was on the river?" he asked in surprise.

"Lived and died on it," I replied. "And you work from Pelican Stairs?"

He nodded. I indicated the notebook. "Yes," he said.

I knew the location. "And when did you find the body?"

"Yesterday, just afore noon. I was coming ashore, and my hook caught on something. I couldn't free it by myself, so one of the other lads came onto my boat and we hauled it in together."

"Was the body just as I see it now? No boots?"

The lighterman's eyes flicked to my notebook and he thought for a moment. "I didn't take no boots, sir."

I left it at that. "And so you carried the body here?"

"Yes. All bodies found in this part of the river are brought here first, on account of the cold back room. One of the ship's constables was drinking in here, and he said he thought there might be a reward – he'd seen something posted on a board near Execution Dock. About a man with a limp. And this body, with the legs... Two guineas he said."

He looked at me hopefully.

"Well, the body is certainly that of the schoolmaster Mr Dyer. I knew him."

The lighterman looked stricken. "Oh sir, I had no idea he was a friend. My condolences." And he screwed his cap even tighter.

"Thank you, Mr Redbridge. He was not a friend exactly, but he leaves a wife and six children who will feel his loss most keenly." Redbridge shook his head sorrowfully. "When you brought the body here, did anyone ask you to put a piece of paper in the coat pocket, or did you see anyone do that?"

The lighterman looked surprised. "Paper, sir? No."

I closed my notebook. "Tell me, Mr Redbridge. Did you notice anything about the hands of the dead man?"

"Oh aye – like claws they were," he nodded vigorously.

"And what does this make you think, Mr Redbridge?"

"Think, sir?"

"Like me, Mr Redbridge, you have seen plenty of drowned bodies. Do you think Mr Dyer went into the water willingly?" I put my head on one side.

Redbridge looked down and shook his head slowly. "No, sir, I do not."

"And you'll be telling me next that no-one has gone to tell Sarah about her husband," said Martha, once I had finished recounting what I had seen at the Red Cow. She stood at the range, stirring a pot slowly as she listened.

"Well, I will call on Mr Conant this evening; he will want to know that we have found Dyer, and will need to make arrangements for the reward to be paid to Redbridge. After that I could walk round to see her." I did not relish telling Mrs Dyer that she was now a widow, and I daresay my reluctance was apparent in my voice.

"I think perhaps she should hear it from another woman," said Martha after a moment. I looked at her gratefully. "I just hope her sister is still there, to help with the children. Sarah is not robust at the best of times, and this news is sure to bring her very low."

"Martha," I said, biting my lip as I tried to find the right words. "Martha, about Dyer." I caught her arm as she passed me. "Sit down, my love – there is something you need to know." She put down the pot she was carrying and sat on the edge of her seat, watching me intently. "When a person drowns, there are three possible explanations. First, an accident: perhaps after too much drink, or in bad weather, a person can slip and fall into the water. I think this is very unlikely, as Dyer would have had no cause to be in Wapping."

"But the current," suggested Martha. "Perhaps he fell in somewhere else and the river carried his body downstream."

I shook my head. "From the condition of the body, we know that it fell in only a short while before it was recovered – there was no time for it to move far." She nodded. "Second, self-murder."

Martha's hand flew to her mouth. "The poor man! A debt is bad, certainly, but surely not all that bad – and poor Sarah. Oh Sam, not another one."

"No, not another one, my dear. There was nothing to suggest it. He was still wearing his coat." She looked puzzled. "For some reason, people who drown themselves often take off their outer garments and leave them behind. Not always, but often enough for it to be a good indication." I paused. "And so the third explanation we have is murder by another hand." Martha's eyes grew wide, but she said nothing. "And I am afraid that I think this the most likely explanation. His hands, the hands of the corpse, they were like this." I made claws of my hands. Martha stared at them. "This suggests that he was trying to resist, trying to grab on to someone or something to keep from drowning. And then there was this." I reached into my pocket and handed her the note that I had found on Dyer's body. She read it and looked up at me.

"What does it mean, Sam? What are the birds?"

I told her what Wontner had told me about magpies, and I reminded her about the man in the canary waistcoat, and lastly I described my visit to the Aviary. "All birds, you see," I said.

"But this means that whoever murdered Mr Dyer knows that someone is piecing together the puzzle, and wants to send them a warning." I nodded. "Oh Sam, it really is Georgie Mac, isn't it?"

I nodded again. "I think Dyer was murdered to scare me off." I finished and sat silently. Martha reached across and took one of my hands in both of hers and stroked it gently. "But I think it best that you do not mention this to Sarah."

Martha looked at me sharply and withdrew her hands. "Why on earth not?"

"Well," I floundered around for what to say. "She will find it frightening. She may think that whoever murdered her husband will threaten her too. Although I think it unlikely. She has nothing that they would want."

Martha shook her head. "Oh Sam, how little you men understand us. Death does not frighten us nearly as much as it frightens you. Women see enough of it to know that death is not half so terrifying as life." She stood and looked out of the window for a short while before turning back to me, tears in her eyes. "Sam, if – God forbid – you were to die from home one day, and someone came to my door with the news, I would want to know that your last thoughts were of me, and that your last action was to use every ounce of strength left in you to cling on to our life together. It is far better for Sarah to know that her husband died reluctantly, than to think that he chose to leave her or was happy to do so."

The image of Henry Dubois's young widow, looking at me with her dark eyes and begging me to help her understand why, leapt into my mind, and I knew Martha was right. I beckoned her to me, pulled her onto my lap, and held her as tightly as I could.

CHAPTER THIRTY-THREE

The man with seven names

MONDAY 10TH OCTOBER 1825

John Wontner stood as Wilson and I were shown into his office.

"Thank you for coming so quickly, Sam," he said, referring to the note he had had delivered to us a couple of hours earlier. "I think you will be glad you did." He smiled at Wilson. "William, isn't it?" Wilson nodded. "And how are you coping with our Constable Plank and his unusual ways?"

"My ways are not unusual," I protested. "They are merely – determined."

"Well, William, you could certainly do worse than follow his example." Wontner shuffled some papers on his desk but made no effort to enlighten us as to the purpose of his summons. "Ah!" he said as there was a knock at the door. "Here he is."

The door was pushed open, and in came a man who reminded me of nothing so much as a bank clerk: neat, modest, unassuming. He removed his hat, brought his heels together, and made a half-bow in our direction.

"Constables," said Wontner, "may I present to you Mr Samuel Fountain. And Mr George Welton, Mr Henry Samuels, Mr..." he glanced down at a paper on his desk, "Mr Isaac Williams and Mr Charles Fredericks. Have I left out anyone?" he asked the man.

"Frederick Welton," he replied.

Wilson was writing as fast as he could in his notebook.

"And your actual name?" prompted Wontner. "The one bestowed upon you by your poor doting mother?"

"Walter Ambrose."

"Thank you," said Wontner. He turned to me. "Mr Ambrose provides a very particular service to certain people. Mr Ambrose, perhaps you could explain."

The man with many names twisted his hat in his hands. "Well, sometimes a gentleman will wish to be rid of a nuisance – a troublesome business partner, perhaps."

"Or a magpie who has become too greedy," interjected Wontner.

"And I assist with that," said Ambrose. Wontner made a circular motion with his hand to encourage him.

"I accuse the man of theft and have him arrested and taken to the Old Bailey," he finished in a rush.

"Where, more often than not, our man is found guilty and sentenced to the scaffold, or – if he is lucky – transportation. Either way, he is no longer a nuisance," explained Wontner. "But there is more, is there not, Mr Ambrose?" Ambrose looked, if possible, even more miserable, but said nothing. "Our friend here has been working hand in glove with one of your own, Sam. A corrupt constable. Mr Ambrose reports a theft, the constable arrests the poor soul, both appear as witnesses – for what could more respectable and credible?" He indicated Ambrose's sombre dress. "They then split the fee that Mr Ambrose charges for this obliging service. Unfortunately for Mr Ambrose, his constable friend has been unmasked – and was only too quick to pull Mr Ambrose down into the mire with him. And like a man in quicksand clutching at a rope, Mr Ambrose here has in his turn thrown us the name of one of his clients: Mr George Macintosh."

"Dear, dear," I said, shaking my head sadly. "What a sorry tale this is. Have you taken full notes of everything, Constable Wilson?"

"I have, sir, yes," said Wilson.

"And what felonies, in your opinion, would be of interest to the judge in this matter?" I asked.

"Encouraging and concealing criminals," replied Wilson. "Falsely charging another with a felony. Compounding a felony."

I looked at Wontner, who nodded vigorously. "Oh, at the very least, constable – at the very least," he said.

I must admit that I started to feel some compassion for Ambrose, who looked as if he might collapse at any moment. He was a despicable creature, to be sure, but it is never pleasant for a man to find the world turning against him.

"But perhaps, Mr Wontner," I said as though the thought had just occurred to me, "we could make it known to the judge that Mr Ambrose has been most helpful to us in our pursuit of Mr Macintosh, an altogether more serious felon."

Ambrose turned his sharp face to me, as a weasel will twitch its nose towards a chicken house.

"A vicious felon, not above breaking the fingers of a constable." As I said this, Wilson held up his left hand; the binding was gone, but you could see from the slight bend in the fingers that damage had been done. "A cruel man, capable of murdering those whom he suspects have betrayed him. Capable of holding a crippled man under the water until he drowns."

I glanced across at Ambrose, and he was pale and gulping. Wontner seemed to consider the matter. "But how could Mr Ambrose be of such help to us?" he asked innocently.

"Well," I said, "Mr Macintosh is a debtor, is he not? Which means that he has creditors. Now, some of these are known to us already, but I would very much like to know the full extent of his financial commitments. And I think that Mr Ambrose, with his friends in dark places, is perhaps the man to enlighten us. After all, the chances are that one of Mr Macintosh's men is at this very moment reporting that he has just seen Mr Ambrose in the company of a prison keeper and two constables. A wise man would think very carefully about who is likely to be more forgiving: a judge, or Mr Macintosh."

CHAPTER THIRTY-FOUR

Due diligence

WEDNESDAY 12TH OCTOBER 1825

The scorching days of July were a distant memory, and I was glad to escape the slicing autumn winds. At the counter, Tom Neale shook his head. "It's going to be a bad winter, Sam – snow by the end of the month, I shouldn't wonder."

"Snow in October?" I laughed in disbelief. "Is my visitor here yet?"

Tom jerked his head in the direction of the back office. "As instructed, I did not make him welcome."

As I opened the door to the office, the man at the table stood to greet me. He was young, as Freame had guessed he would be, but would not age well. His plump face and petulant lips suggested an over-indulgent mama, but the chewed nails on the hand he extended to me told me that recent months had not been so easy.

"Edmund Rawlings," he said. "Mr Freame suggested that it might be wise for me to come and see you."

I had Freame's note in my pocket, delivered the previous afternoon: "I have found your man. He will be with you at nine in the morning, with all of the Macintosh records."

My eyes strayed to the ledger in front of Rawlings on the table, and he put a protective hand on it.

"Mr Rawlings," I said, sitting and indicating that he too should sit. "I take it that Mr Freame has explained why I want to see you." He nodded. "I have something of an interest in felonies of a financial nature; last year I was involved in unravelling some of the complexities of the Fauntleroy case." Rawlings swallowed hard and put a hand to his throat. "Tell me about your banking house, Mr Rawlings."

"My banking house?" he stammered.

"Are you the managing partner, for instance?"

"Yes, yes I am. Last year my father, who was the managing partner before me, had an attack of apoplexy. He survived but the bleeding has left him weak, and he is confused in his mind. I was already working at the bank so I stepped into his shoes."

"Was Mr Macintosh a customer at the bank under your father?" I asked.

Rawlings shook his head. "No: about a month after I took over, one of my clerks told me that he knew of an important customer who was unhappy with his current banker and looking for a new one."

"Had the clerk been with you long?"

"No, only a fortnight – why do you ask?"

"I ask, Mr Rawlings, because Mr Macintosh has taken you for a fool. Men like him pay a good deal of money so that others will keep an ear to the ground on their behalf. He will have heard of a banking house being taken over by a greenhead, and he will have seen a way to turn your inexperience to his advantage. Your new clerk is one of his men, I am certain, and the introduction of Mr Macintosh part of a clever plan." I stood up and leaned on the back of my chair. "Let me guess the rest, Mr Rawlings. Mr Macintosh came to see you, and after a meeting during which he sidestepped all of your questions and told you about his business in only the most general of terms, he said that you were exactly the right banking house for him, and that – in order to secure your personal attention – he would be willing to pay more generous fees than your other customers." Rawlings looked rather nauseated but nodded. "He then sent someone round with a ragbag of business papers, and asked you to rationalise them into correct banking standards." I walked over to a cupboard, unlocked it, took out the ledger that Wilson had obtained, and placed it softly on the table. "In this ledger."

The banker's eyes widened. "But where did you...? Mr Macintosh has been furious – insisting that I must have misplaced it."

"And if we open both ledgers, Mr Rawlings," I opened our ledger while he opened the one he had brought, "we can both see that the writing in them is the same. Your hand, Mr Rawlings." He slumped back in his chair.

"I am not sure quite when you realised that your customer was a scoundrel, Mr Rawlings – but whenever you did, it was too late for you to do anything about it. By then you were devoting so much time to him that your other customers, your honest customers, had grown weary of your neglect and taken their business, their honest business, elsewhere. Once Macintosh knew that you were entirely dependent on him – his tame clerk would have kept him informed – he started asking you to do more and more while paying you less and less. Until we reach today, Mr Rawlings," I sat down and looked him full in the face, "when a corrupt banker is brought before a magistrate's constable to admit to what he has done."

"It's all true," said Rawlings, in a voice so quiet that I had to lean forward to hear him. "Just as you said. By the time I realised what kind of man he was..." He shook his head miserably. "What will happen to me, constable?"

"Well, concealing a criminal is a capital offence." I find that giving a man a sniff of the noose does focus his attention. "But I am a reasonable man, Mr Rawlings. If you can give me your assurance that, from now onwards, you will lead a blameless life, and that you will run your banking house with strict adherence to both moral and legal standards," Rawlings was nodding vigorously, "then I think I can persuade the magistrate that you will be of more use to us alive than dead."

"Constable, my behaviour will make that of the Clapham Saints look giddy." The banker leaned forward in his eagerness to convince me.

I bit my lip to stop myself smiling at the thought of Rawlings living a more pious life than Mr Wilberforce and Mr Thornton. "Mr Rawlings, sainthood will not be required; I was thinking more of your skill as a banker. What I need from you – and your ledger – is a list of the creditors whose demands are responsible for Mr Macintosh's imprisonment in the Fleet." I handed him a sheet of paper and pushed a pen and inkwell towards him. "Please: write them here, along with the amounts owing."

I sat quietly while Rawlings consulted his ledger and wrote six names and figures on the sheet and then passed it back to me. I read it, and then handed him another blank sheet. "And now, on this sheet, Mr Rawlings, please write the details of Mr Macintosh's real creditors – the ones whose names were not supplied to the court." The banker looked shocked and started to protest, but I held up my hand. "Saint or sinner, Mr Rawlings, saint or sinner."

I left him alone in the office with his ledger and his conscience, and when I returned ten minutes later he was sitting, head bowed, the ledger closed in front of him. Waiting for me was a sheet of paper with eight more names on it, and this time the amounts owing were much, much larger.

"Thank you, Mr Rawlings," I said, tucking both sheets of paper into my pocket. "I will be sure to mention to the magistrate how helpful you have been. And might I suggest that in future you choose your customers more carefully – you know what they say about lying down with dogs."

CHAPTER THIRTY-FIVE

The smiles of two ladies

THURSDAY 13TH OCTOBER 1825

Martha was stirring the porridge so I took advantage of her distraction to plant a kiss on the back of her neck. She squealed and batted me away.

"You're in a cheery mood this morning," she said, filling a bowl for me and putting it before me.

"Well, it's not every day that a man knows that he is going to make two women happy – three, if he counts his own wife," I said.

"What are you talking about, Sam?" she said, laughing despite herself. "What could you possibly do today to make three women happy?"

I winked at her. "There's many a trick in an old dog, Mrs Plank."

For my first visit of the day, I made sure that my hat and coat were well brushed – prompting more teasing from Martha, of course – and walked through the morning bustle to St James's, calling in at Great Marlborough Street on the way to pick up the items that Rawlings had sent round the day before. After the grime and grubbiness of the last few days, I was looking forward to this appointment.

At the grand front door of Walsham Place, I explained to the footman who I was, and he showed me into the morning room where Lady Walsham was waiting for me. She was over-decorated for my taste but I could see that under all the gilding, she was a true beauty, with a pair of grey eyes that could make a man do almost anything. She waited until the footman had left us and closed the door behind him before she spoke.

"Constable," she said, inclining her head. "I understand from Mr Conant that you have news for me with regard to the unfortunate matter on which I consulted him." She indicated a chair alongside her own, and I sat.

"Indeed, Lady Walsham," I replied. "In fact, I have more than news." I reached into my pocket and brought out the small cloth bag that until recently had been kept in the safe at Rawlings's bank. I handed it to her. "I have these items."

She took the bag from me, undid the drawstring and tipped the contents into her skirt. She picked them up one by one until she came to a necklace and gave a little cry of pleasure. I had looked at the pieces myself when they had been delivered, and the necklace – a fairly plain one, with a simple purple stone in a pendant – was to my eye among the least valuable of them.

"I am sorry that they are not all there, Lady Walsham," I said. "I understand from the banker concerned that some pieces have been sold."

She looked at me with a smile that turned her face into that of a young woman, a bride even. "Most of them can be replaced, constable, but this one," she held up the necklace, "this was a gift from my mother on the birth of my first daughter. I have lost both mother and daughter, but when I wear this necklace, they are with me again." She fastened the chain around her neck and kissed the pendant before tucking it inside her fichu. "Thank you, constable – thank you." Her remarkable grey eyes sparkled with tears, and I stood and bowed, leaving her with her memories.

I then made my way to Ludgate Hill, and put my proposition to Josiah Carley. To be honest, it was not my proposition, exactly – rather, one I had borrowed from Mr

Freame – but the lawyer was quick to see the benefit and agreed to accompany me to see his daughter. We knocked on the door of the house in Gerrard Street, and Emily showed us into the parlour. The black hangings had been removed from the paintings and mirror, but an air of mourning still clung to the house and its occupants. Carley had warned me that I would find his daughter much changed, but nevertheless her appearance shocked me.

When she came into the parlour and embraced her father, Mrs Dubois could have been mistaken for his sister rather than his daughter. Her chestnut hair was shot through with grey, beneath her eyes were dark smudges of misery and her mouth was pinched. I tried not to let it show that I had noticed, but she put a hand to her hair as she sat. "Forgive me, constable – I am not at my best. Somehow it seems rather a waste of time..." her voice trailed off.

"Come now, my dear," said her father with forced jollity, much as one might encourage a reluctant horse over a fence. "Come now, we agreed that you would make an effort, for George's sake if nothing else." She smiled a narrow smile but said nothing. "Anyway, Kitty dearest, Constable Plank has some good news. Some very good news."

She looked at me politely, but without much interest – when he robbed Henry Dubois of his money, his dignity and his life, Macintosh also stole the optimism and hope from Kitty Dubois. And for that he would now pay.

"Your late husband made some investments," I began. Mrs Dubois closed her eyes momentarily and gave a very slight shudder. "At the time we thought that he had made a mistake, that he had been deceived – as indeed did your husband himself – but time has shown us all to be wrong. It appears that your husband knew rather more than we gave him credit for."

Carley leaned forward and touched his daughter's hands, which were clasped in her lap.

"Kitty, he said softly, "Henry's investments have paid off. The profit from the scheme has been realised, and his share has been paid out. It comes to you, of course, but I shall look after it for you, and when George is of age I shall teach him the management of it. It is not a vast sum, to be sure, but it is sufficient for you to feel safe in this house for as long as you want to stay, and to light the fire in October should you wish."

Mrs Dubois smiled more genuinely at this; we had all noticed the chill in the room. "Papa," she said, "this means that Henry was not a foolish man. He did not let us down, as he thought. He made a good decision after all. As I always knew he would."

Carley knelt down in front of his daughter and she leaned into his arms.

"Yes, Kitty – it means exactly that."

I left the room quietly. In Carley's pocket was the note that Henry Dubois had left for his wife. Whether Carley returned it to his daughter or not, I knew that Kitty Dubois would remember her husband as a wise and generous man – and restoring peace to a widow's heart was as good a way as I could think of to spend some of Macintosh's money.

CHAPTER THIRTY-SIX

Plus interest

THURSDAY 20TH OCTOBER 1825

Earlier in the week, I had called into a small bootmaker's shop just off Conduit Street. The narrow premises were rendered even smaller by the shelves reaching to the ceiling, filled with boxes and lasts, and the alacrity with which the bootmaker propelled himself from the workroom at the back into the shop suggested that customers were not as numerous as he would like. His face fell a little as he took in my uniform, but through force of habit his gaze dropped to my feet.

"Some new boots, constable?" he asked hopefully. "A fine sturdy pair to see you through the winter, and several more to come?"

I shook my head. "Mr Benjamin Humphries?" He nodded. "Then I have the right man," I said, extracting a folded piece of paper from my pocket and consulting it. "On the sixteenth of December last, you made an application to the court citing an outstanding bill for a Mr George Macintosh." I glanced up at Humphries, and his welcoming smile faltered. "Is that right?"

"Yes, yes, I believe that was the date."

"An outstanding bill in the amount of," I looked down at the paper again, "eleven guineas."

"If you say so," replied Humphries, the knuckles of his hands showing white as he clutched the counter of his shop.

I put the paper on the counter and reached into another pocket. "I am here to repay that debt." I took out a purse and carefully counted out eleven guineas. I then added a few more coins, saying "Plus interest, of course." Humphries stared at the money but made no effort to take it; in fact, he put his hands behind his back.

I waited. "Mr Humphries, is there a difficulty?" He shook his head. "Mr Macintosh has found some forgotten reserves, and of course the creditors named in the court records have first claim on them. It is all quite normal, I assure you. I have here a petition prepared by Mr Conant, the magistrate on whose orders I call on you today, and all you need to do is sign it to say that the debt has been discharged to your satisfaction."

Humphries looked at the paper as though it were a snake poised to strike. "And what will happen then?" he asked quietly.

"Well, I have several more creditors to visit, but once I have all the required signatures, the petition will be presented to the relevant authorities, and Mr Macintosh will be freed."

Humphries swayed on his feet. "Freed? How soon?"

"With any luck, by the end of the week," I said jovially. "They're queuing up for rooms at the Fleet, you know – they'll be glad to be rid of him."

I tapped the paper with my finger, and Humphries reached under the counter for a pen. He scratched his name with a trembling hand. I waited for the ink to dry, then retrieved the paper, folded it and put it back into my pocket. As I closed the shop door behind me and glanced in through the window, Humphries was standing where I had left him, staring at the pile of coins on his counter.

"And it was pretty much the same with the other five creditors too," I said to Mr Conant as he read through the petition that evening. "As well as the bootmaker, I was able to scare the life out of a butcher, an inn-keeper, a lawyer's clerk and two physicians. None of them seemed at all pleased to have their debt repaid, even with interest."

"I daresay they are all wondering what Macintosh will do about their investments now," said the magistrate. "Pretending to be a creditor in order to help a man to, in effect, commit himself to the Fleet is an interesting way to pay off a debt – but now that the arrangement has been undone, they no doubt fear that it will all start up again."

"The threats, the demands for more money..." I nodded. "But I rather think that Mr Macintosh will have more pressing concerns this time tomorrow."

Conant looked at me steadily, but said nothing. It was one of the pleasures of working with such a man: he knew when to ask questions, and when to leave well alone. He looked back down at the petition, then dipped his pen and added his signature, together with the date. He blotted the paper carefully and handed it to me.

"Tomorrow?" he asked.

I nodded. "As soon as possible, I think. Time for Mr Macintosh to taste a few drops of his own medicine."

CHAPTER THIRTY-SEVEN

The first snow of winter

FRIDAY 21ST OCTOBER 1825

The next morning Wilson and I walked to the Fleet. The draymen's horses stamped and shook their heads as they stood while carts were loaded and unloaded, their harnesses jingling and their breath clouding in the air. Alongside the prison gate in Farringdon Street was an arched barred window, opening into a room within. Above the opening was inscribed in stone, "Pray remember the poor prisoners, having no allowance". A bearded man, sitting in the shadows inside the barred room, was chanting the same words over and over again in a haunting monotone, like a prayer in church, and a small wooden box sat on the windowsill.

"Madness," I said to Wilson as I reached into my pocket for a coin. "This is what happens when a man is thrown into prison for debt: he cannot earn, he has to pay his garnish, and so a respectable man becomes a beggar by court order."

We explained our business to the turnkey who stood sentry just inside the heavy, stone-framed doorway, and he took the signed petition from us and in turn handed it to a young lad who ran off across the prison yard with it. Wilson and I took a seat on a bench by the wall in the front courtyard, and waited. The high curved wall reared up behind us, the five-storey brick-built prison buildings were in front of us, and the semi-circular yard between them was rather like a market-place. Men gathered in small groups, smoking and chatting, passing newspapers between them. A lively game of skittles was taking place in one corner, while two men were engaged in a lacklustre boxing bout in another. People came and went in constant movement, entering and leaving the yard, running up and down the narrow staircases of the blocks, slamming doors, laughing, crying – like any street anywhere, except that this one was home only to debtors.

After half an hour, the young lad returned and gave the petition back to the turnkey. He glanced at it, then beckoned me over.

"Do you want to deliver the good news in person?" he asked with a smirk.

I shook my head, taking the petition from him. At the bottom, the warden had written "All debts discharged – approved for release" and signed his name, William Brown. "No: I'm happy to wait for the warden's message to reach him," I said, and Wilson and I left the courtyard. Outside in Farringdon Street I pulled out my watch, and ran my thumb over the recently-acquired dent in its case.

"The warden sends round the release notices at two o'clock each afternoon," I explained to Wilson. "So Mr Macintosh should be taking his first sniff of freedom at about three. No need for you to wait all that time; you head back to the office."

Wilson agreed and strode off; like all young men, he had little patience for waiting, and our half-hour in the prison yard had made him restless enough. It was now even colder, and I did not relish standing outside for three hours, so I ducked into a coffeehouse, found myself a quiet table away from the door, and settled down with a warm drink and a good selection of newspapers of all political persuasions.

The bells of St Bride's tolled half past two, and I pulled my coat tightly around my neck before venturing back out into the cold. The smell of snow was in the air; Thomas Neale had been right after all. This time I did not go into the prison yard, but instead stationed myself opposite the gate. The bells marked a quarter to, and then the hour, but there was still no sign of Macintosh, and I began to wonder whether his influence was such that he could ignore a petition signed by a magistrate and the warden. But just then I saw him; with his height, his bright hair – albeit now streaked with grey – and that scar he was unmistakeable. He carried a bundle under his arm and wore a thick coat, a warm cap and good boots. But he was alone.

I watched him as he stood outside the prison gate. He sniffed the air like a dog, then turned up his collar, hunched his shoulders, and set off towards the river. I followed him for a little way before lengthening my stride until I was alongside him and fell into step with him. I could feel him stiffen; a man who lives among criminals for years develops a sixth sense for trouble.

"Hello Georgie," I said, and his hand slipped into his pocket. "No need for that, now, is there?" I said mildly.

He stopped and looked at me, and at my constable's uniform.

"Are you here to arrest me?" he asked, a note of hope in his voice.

I shook my head. "Oh no. You're free, Georgie. The debts lodged against you have been paid off. Of course, there may be other people who feel that they have a claim on you, but have little appetite to involve the courts in your, well, shall we call them arrangements. I daresay they will be particularly pleased to hear that you are at liberty again, so that they can discuss the matter with you in person. Word is being sent to them this very afternoon."

He stared at me a moment longer. "Do I know you?" he asked.

"Samuel Plank," I said levelly. "You might remember my brother. Joseph Plank."

He frowned and then shook his head. "Joe Plank, from Wapping? All those years ago?"

I nodded.

"But you're a..."

"A constable, yes, working for Mr Conant in Great Marlborough Street. A long way from Wapping, to be sure."

Macintosh shook his head again. "I always thought you'd end up a lighterman, like your father."

"I like to think that the world has a certain balance to it, Georgie. Wapping spawned you – and it spawned me."

Realisation dawned in his eyes. "It was you," he said, pointing a finger at me. "You made them all sign to say that their debts had been repaid."

I shook my head. "They had no choice, Georgie – the debts were repaid."

"But who would repay my debts?"

"You did, Georgie." It was my turn to reach into a pocket. "Do you recognise this?" I pulled out the ledger. He made to grab for it but I was too quick. "Everyone we spoke to has been most helpful – your magpies, your banker – all were quick to see that it was the right thing to do." I tucked the ledger back inside my coat. "I'll keep hold of this, I think: there are still a few more matters for me to address."

Macintosh stared at me. "They'll be back," he said defiantly. "Word will get out that Georgie Mac is recruiting."

I nodded. "You may be right, Georgie. But when it comes to it, where are they now you need them?" I looked around me. "Where are all your business partners? Your friends? You cannot buy loyalty, Georgie – you can only earn it."

The bells tolled once more, and I thought of Martha, waiting for me at home. This man was not worth a minute more of my time. I simply tipped my hat and walked off, but as I reached the corner of Fleet Street I turned back to look at him. George Macintosh was still standing where I had left him, his pathetic bundle clutched to his chest, as the first tiny flurries of snow started to fall.

Just then, a movement on the other side of the road caught my eye. Leaning against a post, positioned so that he could see both me and Georgie Mac, was a man in a long dark overcoat, its collar turned up against the cold and his hat tipped low over his eyes. He made a slight but definite bow in my direction, as though in thanks, and then turned to go. The gusting wind caught his coat, swirling it open, and there it was: the flash of a bright yellow waistcoat.

Glossary

Ackermann's – a print-shop and drawing school established in the Strand in 1795 by German bookseller and publisher Rudolph Ackermann

Apoplexy – an old term for a stroke

Bawdy-house – a brothel

Bedlam – the colloquial nickname for Bethlem Hospital, founded in 1247 in London and serving for the last six centuries as a psychiatric hospital, now called the Bethlem Royal Hospital

Bird of paradise – a woman of easy virtue, a prostitute

Blockademan – customs officer

Bubble Act – a piece of legislation passed in 1720, intended to guard against speculation (such as that which

had caused the South Sea Bubble in the same year) by requiring joint-stock companies to be authorised by royal
charter, and (perhaps unwisely) repealed in 1825

Cast up one's account – to vomit

Chamber rent – the rent that prisoners were required
to pay for their prison cells

Childbed fever – an old term for puerperal fever

Chum – a cell-mate in prison

Clapham Saints – a group of influential Christian re-
formers based in Clapham and active between 1790 and
1830, including anti-slavery activist William Wilberforce, economist and banker Henry Thornton MP, and
writer Hannah More

Commitment fee – the fee payable by a prisoner to the
keeper on entry to the prison

Constable – an officer working for a magistrates' court,
whose main duty is to arrest people named in warrants
issued by the magistrates

Covent Garden nuns – prostitutes working in Covent
Garden

Debtors' committee – in the debtors' prisons, the inmates
would elect a committee to impose fines on prisoners for
infractions of the prison rules

Drachm – an eighth of a fluid ounce

Exeter Change – the popular name for Exeter Exchange, a building on the north side of the Strand, with

an arcade extending partway across the road and with a resident menagerie of wild animals on its upper floors

Flash man – a rogue, a conman

Flash the hash – to vomit

Garnish – in debtors' prisons, garnish is the fee paid by new prisoners to the debtors' committee on arrival; in other prisons (such as Newgate) the payment of garnish to the warder will mean that the prisoner is not shackled in chains but allowed free movement of his limbs, as well as afforded other comforts

Gentleman of the back door – homosexual

Greenhead – an amateur, a beginner

Incognita – a woman of easy virtue, a prostitute

Irish Ordinary – what we would now call a "greasy spoon" café, known for simple, cheap meals of meat and potatoes

Jarvey – driver of a hackney coach

Ladybird – a woman of easy virtue, a prostitute

Lighter – a flat-bottomed barge, used for transporting cargo between larger vessels and the shore

Master's side – most prisons had two areas: the more open Master's side (for prisoners who could pay their chamber rent) and the more harsh and restrictive common side for poorer prisoners

Meet one's vowels – to pay what is owing on an IOU

Mudlark – someone who scavenges in river mud for items of value

Pink – a fashionably dressed person, a dedicated follower of fashion

Rookery – a city slum

Sticks – furnishings

Tap room – the beer room in a prison

Threepenny ordinary – a set meal of meat, broth and beer, costing threepence

Toper – drunkard

Trifle disguised – slightly drunk, tipsy

Whiddler – an informer

Thank you for reading this book. If you liked what you read, please would you leave a short review on the site where you purchased it, or recommend it to others? Reviews and recommendations are not only the highest compliment you can pay to an author; they also help other readers to make more informed choices about purchasing books.

ABOUT THE AUTHOR

Susan Grossey graduated from Cambridge University in 1987 and since then has made her living from crime. She advises financial institutions and others on money laundering – how to spot criminal money, and what to do about it. She has written many non-fiction books on the subject of money laundering, as well as contributing monthly articles to the leading trade magazine and maintaining a popular anti-money laundering blog.

Her first work of fiction, also featuring Constable Sam Plank, was "Fatal Forgery". "The Man in the Canary Waistcoat" is her second novel.

Printed in Great Britain
by Amazon

40249096R00172